JULIE HALPERN

DON'T STOP NOW

For Amy

e still have a long

SQUARE
FISH

FEIWEL AND FRIENDS • NEW YORK

SQUARE
FISH

An Imprint of Macmillan
175 Fifth Avenue
New York, NY 10010
macteenbooks.com

Square Fish and the Square Fish logo are trademarks of Macmillan and
are used by Feiwel and Friends under license from Macmillan.

Square Fish books may be purchased
for business or promotional use. For
information on bulk purchases,
please contact the Macmillan
Corporate and Premium Sales
Department at
(800) 221-7945 x5442 or by
e-mail at specialmarkets@
macmillan.com.

Halpern, Julie,
Don't stop now / Julie Halpern.
p. cm.

Summary: Recent high school
graduates Lil and Josh leave Illinois for
Oregon seeking Lil's sort-of friend Penny, who
faked her own kidnapping to escape problems at
home and an abusive boyfriend, but Lil also wants to find
out if she and Josh are meant to be more than friends.
ISBN 978-1-250-06450-9 (paperback) / ISBN 978-1-4299-6594-1 (ebook)
[1. Best friends—Fiction. 2. Friendship—Fiction. 3. Runaways—Fiction.
4. Automobile travel—Fiction. 5. Abused women—Fiction. 6. Family
problems—Fiction.] I. Title. II. Title: Do not stop now.
PZ7.H1666Don 2011
[Fic]—dc22
2010048406

Originally published in the United States by Feiwel and Friends
First Square Fish Edition: 2015 • Book designed by Becky Terhune
Square Fish logo designed by Filomena Tuosto

10 9 8 7 6 5 4 3 2 1

AR: 4.9 / LEXILE: 820L

For Amy

Not too much. We still have a long way to go.

CHAPTER ONE

I did it," Penny's voice whispers on my voicemail. Confused, I push the button to replay. "I did it." That's all she said. According to Robot Phone Woman Time Keeper, Penny called at exactly 4:47 a.m., a rather unacceptable time to call anyone on a Saturday morning, and most certainly not on the Saturday morning after the Friday that was our last day of high school EVER. Because it is the first Saturday of the rest of our lives, finally past all of the clique clack crud of high school, I allow myself to sleep past my mother's acceptable sleep hour of exactly 11:59 ("At least it's still morning") until 1:43 in the afternoon. Which makes me approximately nine hours too late to stop Penny.

How did it become my responsibility to help this pathetic soul anyway? We weren't ever friends until this past year, and even then only by default. I had no choice really, unless I wanted to be a total hag by not asking her to join us at the Lunch Table of Misfit Toys, dubbed so by our paltry group of seniors in lunch period 8, who were so placed because we chose not to stress ourselves out with AP classes, resulting in a more pliable schedule for the admin to have their way with. Instead of the race for the maximum number of AP credits possible, I selected some easy, breezy independent studies of things I actually enjoy doing, like Creative Writing and Photo. Why bother with the AP BS anyway? So you can graduate college early? No thanks. I breezed through my senior year like I plan to breeze through this summer, living off the fat of the land that is my bat mitzvah savings, and just chilling out. No worries. Or at least, that was the plan.

"I did it." Who leaves a message like that? Who is so paranoid that they have to be so cryptic? If this wasn't day one of my Summer of Nothing, I might be in a hurry to figure this out. But first: breakfast. Or lunch, really. Snack? Lack, or lunk maybe. It is a bowl of cereal, whatever it is. I like to fancy myself a cereal connoisseur. Today, slightly out of it and in need of substance *and* energy, I mix some Frosted Mini-Wheats with Cookie Crisp, and throw in a few Craisins for fruit and texture. I shake up the skim milk, splash it on, toss around the cereal pieces with a spoon to make sure each piece is coated with milk, and plant myself in front of the computer. Then I second-guess it. Maybe I don't want my lunk interrupted by the possibility of more Penny drivel waiting on the other side of the screen, so I flip on the TV instead. An actual video is on

2

MTV. Hip-hop or rap or something. Not my scene. But I can't help wishing I had a butt like that girl in the video. I wonder how she buys jeans, though.

"I did it." It's like Penny's voice is floating out of my cereal from between the flakes and the crisps. How did she say it? It wasn't urgent or terrified, like someone calling 911 from under her bed as she waits for a killer to enter her room, nor was it excited or light or distracted or a million other adjectives I can think of. She just sounded flat, like the only reason she left the message at all was to keep a record of her existence.

Before I call Penny, you know, just to clarify things, I decide to call my best friend, Josh. Although, if there's one person who can outsleep me, it's him, and I say this from experience. Sadly the experience is due to the fact that he and I are so platonic that his dad and my mom could give a rat turd if I sleep at his house or he sleeps at mine. On the couch, of course. So damn pathetic, then, that I am so madly in love with him. Cliché, touché, but true. I've spent four years waiting for something to happen between us that is more than just sharing a toothbrush when he forgets to bring his own. This summer is the last chance, before I head off to college and he heads off to tour Europe with his band or records the Next Big Thing album he always talks about or possibly moves to Saskatoon to hunt moose. He doesn't know where he'll go, but it sure isn't college. And it's most definitely not in any way, shape, or form

3

dependent on anything I do or anywhere I go. But, damn, I wish it was.

I decide to try and wake him. The phone only rings twice before Josh picks up.

"Heeeyyyy." He sounds awake and happy to see me on the caller ID, which gives my stomach a buzz. I remember once at school when I was talking to some randomer, and Josh came out of the bathroom, me not expecting to see him there because he had Español at the time, and this randomer, upon seeing the two of us see each other, said, "It's like you guys haven't seen each other in weeks. That's how happy you look." And I thought, *Him, too?*

"Good afternoon, sir. May I interest you in a pointless quest?" Josh and I like to go for long walks or drives with fake purposes and dub them quests. Once we spent an entire afternoon "looking for love in all the wrong places," like that super-lame old country song. We looked under rocks, at Ben & Jerry's, in the sand box at Stroger Park. I thought maybe, just maybe, he'd get the hint that love was standing right next to him in a cute pair of cut-offs, but Josh seemed to miss that somehow.

"I'll meet you at Stroger in twenty. And I hope you don't mind, but I have evening stink." Josh isn't much of a fan of showering on a regular basis, which may put off some, but I prefer his sleep smell to some covered-up soap smell any day.

I finish my cereal, drop the bowl in the sink, and tug on a blue bra, blue T-shirt, and jean shorts. Some days I like to be monochromed, just for the hell of it. I brush my teeth, tug my chin-length golden brown hair into a nub of a ponytail, shuffle my way into a pair of flip-flops, and I'm out the door.

The air smells free. Free from class schedules and guidance counselors and hallway politics. High school hell is over.

"I did it." Damn that message. Damn Penny for glomming her way into my life. I wish I didn't care. It's messing with my new freedom vibe.

Three blocks away is Stroger Park, big when I was little and little now that I'm, well, big. Two regular swings, a tire swing, two baby swings, a slide, a wall climb, some monkey bars, and plenty of woodchips to stick in your flip-flops. I always wondered, *Why the woodchips?* It seemed like there would be more woodchip-in-the-eye accidents than woodchips-as-saviors-for-falling-children incidents. Or maybe I just missed them because I was too busy, you know, being a kid.

Josh hangs upside down from the monkey bars, shirtless (as is his summer look), his self-cut, shoulder-length brown hair dangling below him. I try not to ogle, but, damn, he looks amazing without a shirt. How do guys get to look so good without exercising or eating well at all? He's skinny, but not too skinny, and all nice and defined. I exhale a platonic sigh.

"Hey, Lil," he calls and swings himself off the bars, stumbling onto the woodchips. Even graceless, he's gorgeous. "You smell that?" he asks as I approach him, and I sit down on the metal ladder to the monkey bars.

"Well, what do you expect when you don't shower?" I ask.

"No." He chuckles in his slow, slack way. He grabs the high bar closest to me and hangs himself so he can easily kick my knees with his ratty black Chucks. "Not me." He takes a huge sniff of air. "*That*. That smell. The rest of our lives." He grins big and I grin bigger. Our lives are going somewhere away from here. *Like Penny*, I remember.

"I got a message. This morning. From Penny."

"Poor little lamb." Josh always teases me about Penny because I befriended her out of pity, but he plays along, too. We're both too nice to let her go it alone. "What'd she say?" he asks me, still hanging.

I ignore the shoes on my knees. " 'I did it.' " I look up at him and whisper it the same way she whispered to my voicemail.

"Did what?" he asks, but not curious enough. "*It?*" He laughs, although we both know she did *it* a long time ago, thanks to the pregnancy scare aftermath I had to clean up.

"She told me she was going to do something the other

night, before graduation. Only I was just half listening, and you know how morose she can be. Sometimes I just need to block her out if I want to have a bit of fun."

Josh nods and lets the flappy rubber of his messed-up shoe tug on my knee. "So what did she do?" He's more interested now, and now that I've got an audience for the story, so am I.

"If I heard her right . . ." I pause, adding to the tension of the tale I'm about to begin. "Well." Quizzical look. Pause. "I think she may have faked her own kidnapping."

* * *

I hate gym class. I hate wearing this hideous green, too-thin, too-short, too-cold uniform. It stinks. My bad for not taking it home, but I don't even want it to touch my backpack. No one comes near me anyway, so what does it matter. I just wish these shorts weren't so short. Did the makeup cover that purple spot on my leg enough? God, I hope so. I hope no one asks about it. Not like they will.

I wish the boys' gym classes were sharing the gym with us today. No, I don't. I look gross today. Bloated. Must be getting my period. I hope I'm getting my period. God, I hope I get it this time. I don't want Gavin to see me in these shorts. The bruise. Maybe he should see it. No. That might make him mad. Like I'm showing someone. Good thing the boys aren't in here. I'll just sit on the bleachers and hope Dr. Warren doesn't force me to play basketball. Usually if I make a pathetic enough face, she leaves me alone. What is she a doctor of, anyway? Basketball. Did she really go to medical school to just become a gym teacher? Oh, god. She's coming. She wants me to play. She wants me to be on the blue team. I hate the mesh smocks. Who knows who wore this before me?

The blue team. At least there are some nicer people on it. Not those bitches who always laugh at me in the locker room.

And in the hall. When I interrupt them talking to Gavin. What business do they have talking to Gavin? I would kill them all if I didn't know that Gavin loves me more than he could ever love anyone else. That's what he tells me. He wouldn't lie.

This girl Lillian is on the blue team. She's so pretty. So tall. I wish I looked like her. I bet Gavin does, too. I bet she doesn't have a single problem in the world. Isn't she dating that guy Josh? He's so sweet to her in the halls. Arms around her. They look perfect together. Perfect height. Perfect bodies. Perfect lives. I wish I were her.

CHAPTER TWO

Wait. What?" Josh looks at me like he isn't sure he heard me right. "How can she have faked her own kidnapping? How can she fake a kidnapping to begin with? And why would she bother? She's eighteen. What does she need to fake anything for except buying alcohol? And she didn't even have to do that because her parents always left the liquor cabinet open anyway. Remember that night with the Kahlua?" I remember, since I vowed never to allow the tainting of my precious coffee, or anything else for that matter, with alcohol again. "But back to the loon fest at hand. Are you sure that's what she said?"

"I'm trying to remember." I stir some woodchips around with my toe, revealing the dirt underneath. Circle. Circle. Dot. I've just made a woodchip crop circle. "She was sort of going on about Gavin." Gavin being her mostly, sometimes ex, boyfriend. *Mostly* when he wants to be with other girls, not when he wants to be with Penny. Convenient.

"No?" Josh feigns surprise. He sits across the bars from

me now, on the opposite steps. He removes his shoes, no socks, and plucks up individual chips with his toes.

"Yeah, that's why I was only half listening. I feel bad because I know it was more crappy stuff, like him saying how fat she was getting, or how she's not nearly as cute as some of the freshmen. I don't know, it grosses me out to think about it. But I can only tell her he's a dick so many times. I don't even know what she wants to hear from me anymore. Sometimes it's like she looks at me like I'm going to reassure her that he's a great guy. No can do."

"So—fake kidnapping?" Josh attempts to toss a chip with his toes, but it just slips through. He tries again.

I scan my brain for memories. "I think I changed the subject. Asked her about that guy she met on spring break when her family went to Disney World."

"The dude from Portland?" Josh flips chips from his toes toward my crop circle. I think he's trying to make a bull's-eye. I'm always amazed at what goes on up there in his head, how he's able to be so light about some things, serious when I need it, and remember just about everything. Even when it's about some random guy that some not-so-close friend met on a vacation.

"Yeah—Ethan. But when I brought him up, she shushed me. Like, actual full-on librarian shushing."

"You know, librarians don't really shush people as much as you think. That's a stereotype." He tries again with a toe toss. Not even close.

11

I sigh dismissively. "You know what I mean. It was weird. Gavin wasn't even in the room. He wasn't even her *boyfriend* at that particular millisecond, and she's all paranoid that he's gonna hear her talk about another guy. Which she has every right to do." Josh nods, still looking in the direction of his toes. "What's she so afraid of?" I ask, even though I already know the answer.

Josh looks up, chip still stuck between his toes, and asks, "Have you ever seen him in gym class? The guy's a beast. We were playing soccer, by which I mean I was standing in the goal talking to George, and the six bros in the class were bobbing and weaving and man-slapping one another all over the place, and here comes Gavin out of nowhere with the ball. Slams it right into the net. Dudes behind him are spewing names at me I do not care to repeat, and I'm like,"—he holds his arms up in surrender—" 'Sorry.' Gavin busts up to me, all in my face, 'You got a problem, Turdman?' For which I just answered with one of my patented Erdman looks." Josh's looks are both hilariously ambiguous and full of meaning if you know how to read them. "And he's still in my face. I'm like, 'Look, I'm a pacifist, man. Take your macho crap to someone who gives a rat's ass.' For which he declares me a fag and struts away."

"I am so glad we don't have coed gym," I proclaim. "Or didn't, I mean," and I smile at the thought that I will never be forced to do anything phys ed again in my entire life.

"Point being," Josh tries to get me back on subject,

which is not unusual, "the guy's an unpredictable freak. I'm not saying *I'm* scared of him."

"Of course not," I tease.

"But I've heard some things. Locker room things that weren't meant to leave its sanctity."

"Kind of like Vegas, but not at all fun and definitely more stanky."

"Exactly. But none of it good, and all of it reeking of douchebag boyfriend."

Grrr. Why did I even get myself involved with this charity case of a girl? "So I'm starting to piece this memory together a little more. Penny is bitching about Gavin and another girl. Doesn't want to talk about herself and another guy. Then the music got loud. Michael Jackson, 'Wanna Be Startin' Somethin'.' Everyone starts to dance. I wanted to but had to deal with Penny. Tragic. Still couldn't help myself from moving a little, when she whispers something to me. It was one of those conversations where you nod and pretend to hear everything, just to appease the person. She never turns up her voice volume, even when things are loud around her. Drives me crazy."

"Focus, Lil, focus." Josh manages to flip a chip right into the center of one of my circles. "Yesss!" A small fist pump.

"Um, focus?" I chide. Josh smiles. "I'm thinking she said something about having to leave, but not wanting Gavin to know why or where. Doesn't want to make him mad. Then she mentioned Portland again. And then, maybe

I'm just crazy . . ." Josh nods in agreement. "Shut up. But I think she said that she had this idea. She might have even said 'good idea.' To fake her own kidnapping."

"That doesn't make any sense." Josh tires of his toe-chip game and stands up to hang from the bars again. "I mean, at eighteen you don't even have to run away. You can just *go*. Why would she have to fake her own kidnapping?"

"I'm trying to figure that out. If she was going to run away, she clearly would have said 'run away,' which doesn't sound anything like 'fake my own kidnapping.' That seems overly bizarre for anyone, let alone Penny." I lean forward, grab a particularly large wood chip and begin crossing out the circles with Xs. "But let's just say, hypothetically, that someone, possibly even someone named Penny, does fake her own kidnapping. Why?"

"Because she wants attention?" Josh suggests, dangling.

"But Penny didn't want attention. Not that kind, anyway. Not the kind that would let Gavin in on her tryst with another guy. He'd go ballistic, right?"

"So maybe she'd fake her own kidnapping to take the focus off her and put it on a fake kidnapper?" Josh moves his way onto one bar and back to another, legs bent, trying to keep his six-foot-three-inch frame from touching the scrapey ground. I nod in semi-agreement, and Josh continues, "But that's jacked-up." He crosses the bars now toward me. "Kidnapping gets you *and* your kidnapper a buttload of attention. Media-grade attention."

"Yeah, but I think that's how Penny's head works. I bet she didn't even think of that. It's like every thought she has is based around Gavin. Remember how every time we went to a movie and we'd invite her, she'd have to ask, 'How long is it?' Because she might be expecting a text. So I'd say, 'Just keep your damn phone on,' and she'd be all, 'No, because Gavin freaks on people who text during movies, and I don't want to piss anyone off.' Um, Gavin's not even at the theater, and he's the person you are hoping to get a text from anyway, so why would it matter if you texted him at the movies? And she'd say, 'He knows.'"

Josh lands in front of me and plops himself down on the woodchips at my feet. "So let's put ourselves in Penny's brain." We both shudder. "Penny wants to leave town. She needs to move on from Gavin, distance herself from family, suburban life in general. There's some nice guy in Portland waiting for her. But because of some not-so-nice guy here, possibly psycho, she needs to go away *secretly*. Not of her own volition? If she just leaves, she has to give reasons to everyone—"

"She could just leave without telling. She doesn't have to fake her own kidnapping," I interrupt.

"We're in Penny's brain, remember? If she's kidnapped, well, what choice did she have in getting away? Maybe

15

this is her ploy to get Gavin to actually worry about her instead of making her worry."

I think on it for a minute. "I guess. Still sounds completely absurd. And I don't think she'd really do it, do you?"

"Not sure. But what did she mean then by 'I did it'?" We spend a minute perplexed; Josh allows the summer breeze to sway him. I draw stars in the dirt with the stick.

My cell phone rings, and we both startle. I check the caller ID. "Oh my god." I look at Josh. "It's Penny's home line. It's gotta be her dad."

Josh drops down and puts his hand on my shoulder. "It's probably just Penny, telling you that what she meant by 'I did it' was that she bought a new pair of shoes or something."

I shake my head. "She never calls me from this number. She always calls from her cell. I only know it's her parents' number because they always call me when they're looking for Penny because she refuses to answer her cell when they call."

"Are you gonna answer it? Maybe it's nothing."

But I know it's something. She *did it*. Whatever "it" is. I click the answer button. "Hello?"

16

CHAPTER THREE

Rewind to the beginning of senior year. I'm on my no-AP cruise-control plan. Applied to a handful of colleges with good creative writing departments, but nothing overly ambitious to keep me out. Lots of room for a chill senior year. Figured I'd work hard when I'm actually paying for the classes.

Lando Cronenberg (I know, right?) threw a Labor Day blowout at his parents' condo. Not much of a blowout, considering he has neighbors above and below, and his mom and dad are heads of the condo association. But still, fun enough with the usual crew, a few close friends, Josh, and an assortment of people who know people I like and would say hi to me in the hall or sit near me if no one I liked more were in one of my classes. We were playing dirty Scattergories and eating lots of Lando's patented seven-layer guac when in walks Penny Nelson. Shriveled into herself, long brown hair, floor-length black dress. I guess she could have been classified as emo or goth except that her demeanor and behavior just didn't seem that outwardly expectant. She wasn't doing it for everyone else's attention. Whatever she was doing, in fact, seemed to garner her as little attention as possible. In the three previous years we spent together at school, we never actually spent any time together. Well, that's not entirely true. I can probably go back and look at pictures from any party or show or coffee shop that I went to with a group of people, and she'd be there in the background, holding up a wall.

Lando's Labor Day extravaganza was like any other, except that this time I noticed Penny before she melted into the scenery. Maybe it was the way the light hit her face or the fact that the room was only a little bigger than a shoe box, maybe a boot box, but she looked sort of *broken*. Shadowed and caved-in and unbelievably sad. Gavin, her Neanderthal, was there, too. They walked in together, and the second they entered the room, he beelined for the beer and left her to fend for herself. Not that anyone should be fending when they know everyone in a room. But if what I knew about Penny was any indication, she probably didn't *really* know anybody.

I stood up, climbed over a few floor-seated buddies and grabbed myself some tortilla chips and a scoop of dip. I approached Penny cautiously, as one would to get a closer look at a deer without scaring it off.

"Hey," I said and smiled a closemouthed, not too over the top, but trying somewhat to be warm smile.

"Hey," she replied, with a dart of eye contact and an equally noncommittal grin.

"You want some dip?" I asked. I don't know why, but I felt like it was my duty to get this girl out of her slump and into this party.

She shrugged an answer that I thought meant no, until she reached a ghostly hand toward the chips, grabbed one, and dipped the tiniest corner into the guac. Her fingernails were chewed to the quick, and her deep blue nail polish was chewed along with them. She cautiously brought the tortilla chip to her mouth and bit off the barely green corner.

"Good, huh?" I asked enthusiastically. It felt like I was force-feeding a child. Like, "Choo choo, open wide." I took up a chip of my own, slathered on the dip, and stuffed it in my mouth. Aware of the guac goatee I had just given myself, I looked over at Penny and gave a guaccy grin. That's when she smiled, a real smile, a smile that showed she actually had teeth and made her eyes crinkle and everything, and that's how it all started. It became my goal, my mission, my *quest*, to get this girl to smile again. Even if that meant putting effort into something during my senior year.

The nice thing about including Penny in my periphery of friends was that she wasn't usually available to hang out, so it wasn't always all that different from life BP (before Penny). She was usually so glommed on to Gavin that my friendship with her mostly involved me asking her to hang out and her telling me she was busy. All right. But when she was available because of being ditched or dumped or any other variety of Gavin neglect, she was more or less a tagalong. Because no matter how much we tried to include her, Penny just sort of dragged herself behind us, like a deflated balloon left on a string.

I've had friends who talked about their boyfriends *a lot*, and I'll admit to being that girl once or twice (when my short-lived relationships consumed every bit of my soul, only to turn out to be imposters of shams of relationships and really just mildly amusing grope sessions that ended with little to no conversation and even less admiration. No thank you). But Penny's boyfriend-speak is painful, and constant. And try as I might, nothing I say has changed that. Fight after fight, breakup after breakup, long-sleeved shirts in the middle of Indian Summer . . . She just stayed with him. Even when he wasn't with her.

My friends, the close ones, made it question number two every time we made plans. 1. What do you want to do? 2. Is Penny coming? And based on number two's answer, people might show or not show. Except for Josh. He always showed, at my request, even when he had something better to do. Sometimes even when he had a girlfriend, he was ditching last minute to be there. I should've just dumped Penny, left her behind to do whatever it was she was doing before I took on her charity case (What *was* she doing?), but I just couldn't. She was a quest, after all.

· · ·

I hate sitting alone at lunch. But I hate when people ask me to eat with them. Just leave me alone. Isn't that what my face says? I can't even eat this crap. Where is Gavin? He told me he'd meet me here. It's our lunch table. The farthest one in the corner by the window. He once told me he picked it because it made us feel like we were the only two people in the world. In the lunchroom, at least. He can be so sweet. So romantic. So where is he? I don't want to be alone here. I'll give him three more minutes, and then I'll hide in the library. They leave me alone there. As long as I'm quiet, it's like I'm not even there.

It's been one minute. I wish I'd brought a book. Maybe I should just go to the library now. To get an actual book. But then the librarian might say something about what I'm reading or about this cut on my hand or ask how I am. I hate that question. Why do you care? You don't.

One more minute. Now the lunchroom's getting crowded. That lunch table always looks like they're having so much fun. Lillian from gym class and her gorgeous, perfect boyfriend, Josh. They look so comfortable. Not like she's wondering if he really likes her. If he's going to leave her for someone skinnier or prettier or sluttier. Who would leave her, though? Perfect. I wish I were her.

Three minutes is up. Guess I'll go hide in the library. I hope Gavin doesn't show up and get mad that I'm not here. Maybe I'll just stay one more minute.

CHAPTER FOUR

Hello?" I answered the phone, Penny's home number glowing on the caller ID. Ninety-nine percent sure it would be her father on the other end. I can't say I ever deal much with fathers, especially my own (I've got Selfish Divorced Father Abandonment Syndrome), but Penny's dad is always the one to call me or wave to us while he's watering the lawn or ask when she's going to be home, not her mom. He never seemed that nice or affectionate, but he always had this look of guilty concern on his face. Maybe he knew something was going on with her and never could figure out just how to help her either.

"Lillian, this is Mr. Nelson." Check. "Is Penny with you?" He doesn't sound overly traumatized, just trying to figure out where his daughter is. Which is not at home. But that doesn't mean anything. He probably saw her yesterday, and this is just an everyday, ordinary Penny misplacement.

"Sorry, Mr. Nelson. She's not with me." I feel like I'm

lying, when I'm not at all. I'm not even withholding information, since I don't have any and since there is no need for any information that I don't have to be withheld. All he wants to know is if she is with me. And she's not.

"Oh. OK. Well, if you see her, can you please remind her that she's supposed to watch Annabelle today?"

"Sure thing, Mr. Nelson," I tell him. We say good-bye and I hang up, relieved.

"What did he want?" Josh asks. I stand up, so Josh and I are almost eye to eye. I'm five eleven to his six three; a perfect match if you ask me. Sometimes I even borrow his pants.

"He wanted to know how much ransom is and if I wanted it in unmarked one hundred dollar bills." Sarcastic look from Josh. "I don't know. He was just looking for her. She's supposed to babysit her sister today."

"Shocker," Josh says, and he grips the bar above again to hang.

"Dude, put the pits away," I tell him and step back from the hairy armpit dangling in my face. Not that he smells so bad. "And no, it's not a shocker. Sometimes I think the only reason her parents had Penny was so that they'd have a babysitter for Annabelle. Like *My Sister's Keeper*, but in reverse and without the cancer."

"That almost makes sense," Josh chides. "Let's go sit on the swings."

We walk over to the swing set. Two of the swings have

24

been flung over the top of the bar, so that the seats are so high only a person of, say, approximately six feet could untangle them. "It's our responsibility to undo these, you know," I tell Josh and point to the wrapped swings.

"Why us?" he asks, sounding accused.

"What are those poor kids going to do when they get here and see that two of the swings are out of commission? They're going to have to battle it out for the remaining swing, possibly with a dance-off."

"Or they could just climb up the side of the swing set and whip them down," he argues.

"Just do it," I command. I reach up and grab the black plastic seat with both hands, then give it a good thrust forward and upward so it flies over the top. I duck out of the way, and the seat lands one roll farther down with a jangle. I grab it again and throw it back over. Josh does the same thing next to me. As the swings get lower, it gets more dangerous and inevitable one of us will get hit. I dive away each time the swing flops over the top, while Josh nonchalantly dodges. Once the swings are fully down and the chains are unchinked, Josh dusts off the seat of one swing with his hand and offers it to me. "Why, thank you, sir," I say and sit. He sits on the swing to my right, and we kick off from the ground to start swinging.

"Why does Annabelle even need a babysitter? Isn't she, like, nine?" Josh calls from his place in the air.

"Nine isn't that old, Josh. But I don't know why they

always expect Penny to do it. It's not like she doesn't have stuff to do. And it's not like her mom's ever doing anything. She doesn't even work." Penny's mom, who is always home whenever I go over to Penny's (noted by her gigantic silver Hummer parked in the driveway, but never by an actual sighting) is a QVC addict. When Penny and I first started hanging, she told me her mom watches QVC twenty-four hours a day and orders all of her clothes, shampoo, makeup, jewelry, and food off the TV. I totally thought she was exaggerating, until the first time I entered their house. I arrived at the same time as the UPS guy, and he literally had to take six trips to his truck and fasten his heavy load belt just to carry all her boxes to the door. For Penny's last birthday, her mother bought her, no joke, an olive tree. From QVC. That's how in tune and involved her mother is in Penny's life. Thanks for that olive tree, Mom. I'll be sure to get right on that olive harvesting. Makes me glad I'm an only child with a mom whose crazy work schedule at the hospital means that she's actually happy to see me. When she's around.

"Must be nice," Josh says. "Not working."

"Yeah. And you should know." I pump my legs to catch up to Josh's swing height.

"Not for long. My dad told me yesterday that I have to get a real job or go to college. No way in hell I'm going right back to school, and no way in hell I'm getting my life sucked out of me by a nine to five. Hope it blows over."

Josh has not worked a day in his life, thanks to his

overly spoiling and accommodating (not to mention pretty loaded) dad. Not that I'm bitter, but I wouldn't have minded not having to work the last few summers in cruddy retail jobs to add to the bat mitzvah pot for college. I'm just glad my mom gave me the opportunity to choose what I want to do this summer. I can concentrate on my last summer of nothingness before I commit to becoming something for the rest of my life.

Josh doesn't seem too concerned that he has to commit to something when he yells, "Get out of my bathroom!" I start laughing so hard at the memory of being a little kid and landing in the same rhythm of another swinger and having to yell, "Get out of my bathroom!" What does that even mean?

"But I have to pee!" I scream, and we both begin pumping our legs frantically to go higher.

"We jump on three," Josh calls. I haven't jumped from a swing in forever, and we're pretty high up considering our heights and the fact that the swing set is bucking under the weight of two full-grown teenagers' abuse. I'm game. "One . . . two . . . three!" Josh yells, and I propel myself off the swing, landing shakily on my legs. Josh lands next to me, much less planted, and falls onto me for support. We both topple over onto the woodchips, which, as suspected, do not act as a soft landing pad.

We're out of breath and laughing hysterically, and Josh says, "I think I got a splinter in my boob."

"That's what you get for being in my bathroom," I manage to scold him through my laughs. We're laughing uncontrollably now, when Josh pauses to say, "Your hair looks red today." My hair has its own chameleonic way to it, sometimes more blond, sometimes light brown, sometimes reddish. I didn't even know what to put on my driver's license.

"I like it when it's red," Josh says softly, and leans forward to touch a strand. All laughing stops. He looks into my eyes, or at least makes great eye contact, and I look into his, our eyes both so dark brown, they're almost black. We used to say we must be related. But I shouldn't be thinking what I'm thinking about any relative.

A buzz from the woodchips breaks the brown-eyed trance, and I see my cell has fallen out of my pocket. I pick it up and look at the caller ID. It's an unknown number, which I never answer because I was once suckered into a twenty-minute conversation with an old man named Hoyt who called me by accident, and after telling him I was NOT his long-lost daughter, Erma, about sixty times, I had to fake it and tell him what I'd been doing the last thirty years. Of course I couldn't just hang up. This time around I wait and assume whoever is calling will leave a message if it's anything important.

"You hungry?" Josh asks as he shakes out his shoes for possibly hidden woodchips.

"I could be. What are you thinking?"

"Chocolate chippies?" He slips on his Chucks, and I hear the buzz of my voicemail.

"Sounds good," I say absently, pressing a button on my phone. The voicemail lady blathers on about the time. "Yeah, yeah, I know," I tell her. Then the message begins.

"Hey, Lil, it's Penny," she whispers again, this time rushed and more urgent. "I'm flying out in a few minutes. I just wanted to make sure you got my first message and, um, beg you not to tell anyone where I'm going."

"But I don't really know where you're going!" I yell at the message. Josh looks at me like he's about to ask what's going on, but I shoo him so I can hear the rest of it.

"I don't have my phone, so I'll call you when I get there. Promise you won't tell, OK?" Announcements mumble in the background. "I gotta go. Talk to you later." And she hangs up.

I'm on my knees in the woodchips, trying to make sense of the Penny messages. Josh steps over to me. "May I speak now?" I nod. "What?" he prods.

"That was Penny. She was at an airport. I mean, I assume because she said she's flying out in a few minutes. But she didn't say to where. I wish I was a better listener. I mean, not like I care normally, but this time . . . We would have a lead!" Josh snickers at my detective-speak. "Work with me here. I know she has cousins in L.A. that she was kind of close to as a kid. And she once told me her mom

29

has a sister in Austin, but they never speak. But that Portland guy . . . She seemed to really dig him."

"Enough to fly away into his arms?" Josh considers.

"Maybe." I'm stumped. "She said she doesn't have her cell phone and made me promise not to tell anyone where she's going. Which shouldn't be hard since I don't have a solid idea myself."

"So you're not going to tell anyone what you don't know."

"I don't think I'd tell anyone if I did know anything."

"But you kind of know something." This circular conversation is making my head spin. "You know she's going wherever she's going and you know she doesn't want anyone to know that."

"Right. What?" I feel exhausted by the brain over-exertion when my phone rings. "Maybe that's her," I gasp and fumble with the answer button before I get a look at the caller ID. "Hello?" I anticipate a hushed Penny on the other end. But it's not Penny.

"Lillian? This is Mrs. Nelson." Penny's mom. Something about her voice makes me look around, as if she's somewhere nearby, watching. She doesn't sound like the old film diva that I expected, but more like a tired housewife. "I'm looking for Penny," she says, continuing when I don't reply. "I don't know if I should be worried, but I checked her room to see if maybe she was just sleeping in, and her clothes were everywhere. Maybe that's just how messy she always is and I never noticed. I'm probably just worrying for nothing." That hits me right in the gut. Her mom is already worrying. And she thinks it's for nothing. But it really is for something. That must be that whole mother's intuition thing.

"Do you know where Penny is?" she asks. I try to remind myself of Penny's plea, and I convince myself that everything I do from now on is in Penny's best interest. Remember the Hummer? QVC? The babysitting for a mom who should just be there? I ask myself.

"Um, sorry, no," I finally manage to answer. Can she tell I'm lying with her mother's intuition? Am I even really lying? I don't know where she is at this moment. Not a lie.

"Oh, OK. Do you think she's with Gavin?" She doesn't wait for my answer. "She doesn't want us to call her when she's with him, so I don't even know his number. Do you have it?"

"No, I don't, sorry. We're not really friends." I wonder if she can detect the disdain in my voice.

She doesn't let on, but sounds distracted. "Well, when you see her, can you have her call me?" *When* I see her? Does she think I'm in on this? That I know where to find her? I'm worked up when I realize she just means that I'll probably see Penny before she does, since, well, she doesn't really see Penny.

I nod at the phone before I manage a "No problem." We say good-bye and hang up.

31

Josh is looking down at me, waiting for the story. I stare at nothing. "Penny's mom. Looking for Penny. Don't know where she is, Mrs. Nelson. I'll let you know if I see her, Mrs. Nelson." Josh extends his hand to help me off the ground. I brush woodchips off my knees and note the blemished pattern they left on my legs. Still holding Josh's hand, I say, "We're accessories, you know."

"What? Have you been watching *Law and Order* marathons again?" He squeezes my hand and says assuringly, "Lil, how can we be accessories? As far as her parents know, nothing is even going on. And we don't really know anything anyway. You're making a big deal out of nothing. It'll blow over while we eat our pancakes. No worries."

We walk over, hand in hand, to Josh's car, a surprisingly old and beat-up Chevy Eurosport, boxy and white with slick red and black trim on the sides. His dad has offered to buy him something newer and nicer, but Josh doesn't think he'd look right in a new car. Of course his dad paid for this one, too, but Josh's excuse is that he saved him money. I'm just glad one of us has a car so we can go places other than the local jungle gym.

I slide onto the velvety blue seat, chewing the inside of my mouth nervously. Josh starts the car, and the engine roars like a sports car. He turns to me, puts his hand on my shoulder, and looks into my eyes. "No worries. Right, Lil?"

I'm not so sure.

CHAPTER FIVE

Josh and I are finishing up our Festival of Grease (apple pancakes, chocolate chippies, turkey sausage, hash browns, home fries, and coffee). Breakfast convo consists mostly of Josh selecting the fantasy-tour lineup for his hypothetical band situation this fall. I nod a lot, slurp my coffee, and try to look like I'm listening. ". . . And that's when I stuck my foot up that tiger's butt," I hear Josh punctuate a sentence.

"Wait, what?" I shake my head, confused.

"Yeah, not listening." He sips his coffee and looks away, faux offended. He's wearing one of my favorite T-shirts (forced to put on after the perky hostess politely flirted with him but before the gelatinous manager kicked him out for the no-shirt issue), a Bob Dylan concert T of his dad's, complete with genuine holes and fading from years of love and wear. No Urban Outfitters imposter here. I love how the frayage on the neck highlights his Adam's apple and the barely there sprouts of chest hair that make him mannish enough, but not old man furry. What am I going on about?

I break my thought pattern by stuffing the last bite of apple pancake into my mouth, fully aware that my shorts are already screaming against my loaded stomach. I groan. "Must. Get. Up. Stomach about to connect with booth . . ."

Josh and I stand up to leave, and he drops some cash on the table for the check and tip. I used to think when Josh paid it was something of a date, but not after I watched him pay for everyone else he has ever eaten with. "Thanks for the grub, Dad," I say. Josh wraps his arm around my shoulder, something he does often and not in any way that means anything but good friends, and we walk into the summer warmth.

"What do you wanna do?" I ask, sliding on my gigantic brown sunglasses. Josh and I made a decision a while back when a lot of our friends were "borrowing" designer sunglasses from the mall that we should only purchase our sunglasses from drugstores, thus ensuring that they will always be just a little out of style, but consistently hilarious. Josh's are what we refer to as "dick shades," alluding to the fact that they could be detective/cop sunglasses, but more because they look like something a dick would wear. I check out my reflection in his big, square, silver lenses.

"Why don't we go for a drive?" he suggests. I love being with Josh in the car. Sometimes we drive for hours, going to towns far away just to check out the snack array in their gas stations. Other times we drive nowhere all day, just to watch the town move around. And sometimes we just park and talk. Magic always happens in his car. Well, not *that* kind of magic. At least not with me. And I refuse to prod about any of his past girlfriends, particularly because I know all of them. I don't ask, and he don't tell.

As we drive around, I feel antsy. Something isn't sitting quite right. Maybe it's the chocolate chippy/double potato combo. Or maybe it's the fact that, as much as I love the freedom I have declared for summer, there's still the loom-age of college in the back of my mind. But, really, I'm thinking about Penny.

"I feel like a turdball from outer space," I announce.

Josh turns down the radio, some college station playing obscure and unpleasant ambient noise that Josh thinks is music. "Don't. You made a promise to Penny. That's very commendable in this day and age." Josh must also have Penny on the brain, since he knew what I was thinking about without explanation. Great minds.

"As opposed to another day and age, oh wise one?"

"I'm just saying that she didn't have to trust you and you didn't have to be trustworthy, but you chose to be and that's really cool. I totally respect you for that. Among other things."

"Really?" Compliments are supposed to be warm and fuzzy, but there's no need for my cheeks to feel so heated. Josh's smoothness always catches me off guard. Perhaps it's the fact that he actually causes a complete physical reaction, something I can't hide. But back to the matter at hand. "I don't know what else I could have done. Why would I tell her parents if I knew anything anyway? The only reason they give a crap about Penny is because they're out one babysitter. I'm sure they'll forget all about her once they find a replacement."

"A replacement daughter?" Josh laughs.

"You know what I mean. Penny told me that for her sixteenth birthday, her parents gave her a brand-new Honda Civic. She was so stoked until the follow-up gift was a calendar of all of Annabelle's gymnastic, voice, and piano lessons. She's like Annabelle's personal chauffeur. Hey—speaking of, I wonder if she took her car to the airport." Then they could just find her car, and I'm off the hook, I hope.

"Let's do a drive-by." Josh knows the way to Penny's because he's dropped me off for numerous consolation occasions. She lives in one of the nicer subdivisions in a house big enough to have a three-car garage and enough pimped-out parent cars to play with that Penny always has to park in the driveway.

We drive for five minutes through the gridded streets, homes perfectly alternating gray, tan, white, gray, tan, white, when we turn down Penny's street. Already I can see a swarm of cars down the block. As we creep closer, I recognize they're not just parent cars. There's a police car there, too. Lights on. Two cops stand on the driveway. I watch her mom and dad and Annabelle, wrapped in the mom's arms, talking to the police, a man with a mustache (duh) and a woman with a low ponytail. They both wear sunglasses comically similar to Josh's. Penny's car is there, and the passenger door is flung open.

"I don't want them to see us!" I yell.

"Calm down. They won't see us." Josh is driving slower than the already-slow twenty-five mph speed limit.

"Dude, *accessories*, remember? Go faster!" I'm panicked that if they see me, they'll suspect I know something. Not that I'm chock-full of info, but it's more than they have. Or more than they think I have.

"Chill. If I go faster, they'll definitely see me. If I keep going slow, I'll just look like some nosy neighbor."

"Just get me out of here." I want to duck, but they might see that, too. So I just face Josh and pretend to play with the stereo while minimizing the amount of my face they can see. Thank god for my gigantic Walgreen's sunglasses. "Have we passed them yet?"

"Uh-oh. They're flagging us down. They want me to stop. What should I do?" Josh asks wildly.

I look up, only to see that we're already a block and a half away. Josh is smiling a big ol' cheesy grin. "Turdsicle," I say, relieved. "What do you think the police were doing there?"

"How do you think she got to the airport?" he counter-asks.

"Do you think they saw us?"

"Do you think the cops got their sunglasses from Walgreen's, too?"

"Can you please just get me as far away from Penny's house as possible?"

We drive for a while, and I let the whooshing of the wind competing with the music on the radio drown out my thoughts. The Eurosport has no AC, so open windows are a must. We glide onto the highway, and I relax a little with the speed and distance.

The yellow dashes zip past, and I bite my teeth in between each line, making a clicking rhythm in my brain. We're going so fast that I can't keep up, so I quit and allow my eyes to close.

The carb coma kicks in, and I fall asleep for I don't know how long. I'm jolted awake by the vibrating in my pocket. Damn cell phone. I pull it out and see a phone number, still our area code, that I don't recognize. "Who is this?" I hold the phone in front of Josh's face, and he tries to decipher the number while trying to stay in his lane.

"Not sure," he says. "Just let it go to voicemail." I let it and wait for the message buzz.

"How long was I out?" I ask.

"About an hour. We're in Wisconsin now." Josh laughs.

"We made it across the border," I joke. "Did I miss the Mars' Cheese Castle?"

"Nope. We're just about there." The Mars' Cheese Castle is a landmark just over the Illinois-Wisconsin border. It's actually a major letdown if a castle is what you crave, although cheese fans will not be disappointed. When I was little, I used to believe it was an actual castle built entirely of cheese and inhabited by a glorious cheese-making princess. Josh and I finally stopped there after a day at the Britsol Renaissance Faire last summer, and my cheese fantasy was broken. At least their cheese curds are tasty.

"Shall we stop for some curds?" I ask.

"I gotta whiz," Josh proclaims.

"Then that's a yes?"

We pull into the parking lot, which is packed with cheese enthusiasts. Josh heads to the bathroom while I step inside and browse the freezers of cow-shaped cheddar. I purchase a pack of cheese curds, which is kind of like wet cheese nuggets in a bag. I know it doesn't sound it, but they're really good. Like concentrated cheese.

If I hadn't been here already, I might feel the need to peruse the tchotchkes and cheese tidbits, but once you've seen the inside of this so-called castle, the cheese curds are all you need. I wait for Josh back at the car. I hop in and see my cell phone on the seat where I must have left it. There's a message.

I hit the listen button and pray for a message from old man Hoyt. Instead, I get, "Ms. Erlich, this is Sergeant Sundstrom of the Deer Grove police. I'm calling about Penny Nelson. . . ."

Crap.

· · ·

Waiting outside for Gavin to get out of detention. I need to get home to watch Annabelle, but I don't want to leave without seeing Gavin. It's our end-of-the-day ritual. Even if he has detention, I promised to wait at school to say good-bye, one last kiss before we go our separate ways. He won't come home with me when I babysit, and I won't go home with him. So I'll wait.

Lillian and Josh are in the parking lot. I feel like I know them more now. I see them all the time. Even if we don't actually talk. Now I'm not sure if they're going out. Maybe they're just friends. 'Cause I saw him with Zoe Butterman. But maybe that was on the side. Maybe Lil doesn't know. Maybe I should tell her, and then we'd be friends. Or maybe she'd hate me. So I won't.

Josh's hood is open. Smoke coming out. But he doesn't look mad like that one time that Gavin and I were late for a movie and his car broke down. Ended up busting a window, too, when all was done. Not Josh and Lillian. They're laughing. Laughing at the smoke and the broken car. So instead, they walk. Holding hands. Maybe they are dating. They look so good together.

I watch them until I can't see their perfect, tall, beautiful bodies anymore. I watch the spot where they used to be until Gavin grabs my shoulder and spits his gum into the parking lot.

CHAPTER SIX

After I listen to the message, I'm in stun mode. Penny really did it. Did she do it? She must have done it.

"Your face looks weird," Josh says to me, and I'm too shocked by the message to reply in any sort of annoyed way. "Hello?" he asks, poking my shoulder with his finger.

"We completely underestimated this freak."

"Which freak? That guy waiting in line for the bathroom with all those packages of cheese curds? I'm glad I was ahead of him. Who knows what he planned to do with those things."

"No," I interrupt Josh with a bite. "Don't speak for a minute. I need to process." Josh opens his mouth to say something, then reads the seriousness on my face and shuts himself up. "That was a message from the police. Apparently, Penny's purse was found in her car, with her wallet and cell phone inside, although her license was missing. Her car keys were in the ignition and the driver's door was ajar."

"The door was a jar? But how can that be?" Josh jokes this pathetic joke we've made a million times before, at the absurdity of anyone using the word *ajar*. I only now used it because the cop did, and it's pissing me off that Josh is being so goofy about all of this.

"I'm just reporting what the officer said. The *police officer*? Who called *me* on *my* phone?" I emphasize the words to drill it into his brain that police are now calling me to ask where Penny is.

"Wait—the police called you about Penny. So that means that they think . . . What, exactly?" Josh is more serious, as if he finally recognizes the possible weight of the situation.

"I don't know if they think anything. He said he was calling to let me know that Penny is missing and that if I have any information I should call him."

"But why you? Why'd he call *you*?"

"Because I was the last phone number that Penny called from her cell phone at four thirty in the morning." I sigh at the idiocy of it all. Not only did Penny seriously make it look like she may have been kidnapped—abducted? I don't know what to call it, since she's not technically a kid—by leaving her car, purse, and phone, but she's implicated me by calling.

"So how do we know she didn't actually get taken somehow? Like, if you were going to run away, wouldn't you take your purse? Or at least your phone?" Josh doesn't seem to get the illogical way Penny's brain works. Or doesn't work.

"The whole mad scheme was because she didn't want people to know where she was going. And, I gotta say, I'm sort of impressed. Leaving her purse, the door open. Very believable. But her license was missing, so isn't that like a dead giveaway that she took it out? Who kidnaps someone and is, like, 'I better take their ID in case we need to rent a DVD or something'?" I'm wavering between kind of annoyed and kind of in awe. Annoyed that I'm the keeper of secrets and awed by her follow-through, albeit a shady one. "She's usually so passive."

"If she's truly faking her own kidnapping just so she can get away from her life, I'd have to label that one as passive-*aggressive*. It's like the wussiest thing on earth to not have the balls to say, 'Look, I'm leaving town. Don't follow me, don't try to stop me. I'll call when I feel like it.' But she"—he stutters, incredulous—"she can't even leave a note? Instead, she puts you in the middle of some sort of elaborate kidnapping plot, just so she can get a little love, and she's off roaming the country. How do we know the cops aren't calling you because her parents tipped them off or something? Maybe they think *you* kidnapped her! And you're holding her for ransom and won't take less than an olive tree in exchange for her life," Josh pontificates animatedly.

I know he's kidding, but it's kind of weird that the

police called me. Like, maybe they do think I know something? Because I do. But they don't know that. Or do they?

My cell phone rings again, and I jump. Thank god it's my mom's number that appears on the caller ID.

"Hi, Ma," I answer, relieved.

"Hi, honey. Everything OK?" Mom sounds concerned but like she's trying not to.

"Sure. Yeah. Why?"

"Um, I'm sorry to have to tell you this, sweetheart, but a policeman came by the house looking for information about your friend Penny. It seems, well, she may have been abducted." My mom sounds devastated, like this is the worst news a mom could tell her daughter. I want to give it up, right now, to end this ridiculous plot of Penny's, but something stops me. A big, disgusting, faux-military vehicle in shiny suburban silver (reminiscent of Penny's mom's baby, I mean, *Hummer*), complete with skinny mom in baseball cap, pulls up next to us at the Cheese Castle. The woman gets out, two kids barely visible in the backseat above the auto armor, and says to them, "I'll be right back." Then she closes and locks the door—*beep beep*—leaving the kids in the car. You don't do that. That's Mom 101. I saw this episode of *Oprah* about a mom who left her kid in the car because he was sleeping and she didn't want to wake him, and he died. Dead. Suffocated by hot air. My mom would never do that. But Penny's, I'm not so sure.

"Ma, I don't want you to worry. Don't ask how I

know, but I'm pretty sure Penny's all right. Call it friend's intuition. You have to trust me on that."

"It's good to think so positively, Lil."

"No, Ma, I mean, I know, like, *for sure* that she's fine." I wish she could see my face to read the certainty in my eyes.

"Lillian, is there something you're not telling me?" I'm relieved to hear a bit of the suspicious mom in her voice, like she's starting to believe me.

"Maybe." I laugh a little, trying to reassure her. And myself. "I think there's been a misunderstanding between her and her family, and I don't want you to worry about it."

"Are you sure? Because that policeman . . ."

"I'll call him and straighten things out, Ma. You don't have to get involved at all. No worries. Done," I convince her. And just like that I get an idea in my head of how I'm going to deal with this. "I love you, Mom. I'll talk to you later."

"Love you, too. Be good." And she hangs up.

Josh watches me, one eyebrow raised. "So you're turning Penny in, just like that? Game over?"

"Not exactly," I say guiltily. "I told my mom that so she wouldn't worry." I look over at the Hummer. "Good moms worry," I say.

At that moment, a police car pulls into the Cheese Castle lot. I start a bit, wondering for a minute if they're after me, but this is a Wisconsin state trooper, and I seriously doubt things have gotten this extreme that there's an APB out on me. The cop probably just has to get his cheese on. A female police officer steps out of the car and slams the door. I look over at the Hummer again, windows hardly cracked. "Excuse me, officer." I barely recognize my voice as I walk toward the cop. I catch Josh's panicked expression, knowing he probably thinks what I'm going to do has something to do with Penny. Which it does, albeit indirectly.

"May I help you?" she asks with a twinge of suspicion. I see her eyeing Josh, who's now sitting on the hood of his car, shirtless in his dick shades, dropping cheese curds delicately into his mouth.

"I just wanted to let you know that a woman left some kids in that Hummer over there. And it's kind of hot out, you know?" I want to add that real moms don't leave their kids locked up in environmentally destructive tanks while gallivanting about inside cheese meccas. A real mom would bring her kids in and buy them cheese in the shape of mystical beasts. Or cows.

"Did you see where the woman went?" the officer asks.

"Inside the Cheese Castle." I almost laugh at how absurd that sounds. "She's wearing a powder blue baseball cap," I add.

"Thank you." She nods her head and walks with purpose into the Castle.

"Josh," I say, turning toward the shirtless wonder on the hood. "I don't want to go home."

"Yeah, sure, we can go somewhere else. We got nowhere to be." He plucks a curd out of the cheese water and plops it into his mouth. "Just melt on your tongue, don't they?"

"No." I shake my head. "I mean I don't want to go home today. I think I need to get away, too," I proclaim.

Josh sits up, sparked by the idea. "Where do you want to go?" he asks, mischief glinting off his mirror shades.

"To find Penny," I answer.

. . .

I can't believe it. Lillian talked to me at a party. I wonder if she caught me staring at her. She never talked to me before. I mean, she never really ignored me, but I just figured she was so tall, she looked right over me. People do it all the time, tall or not. But she talked to me. She gave me some food. She smiled at me. Beautiful teeth. Is that weird I think she has beautiful teeth? She does. And hands. Long fingers. Mine are stumpy.

So she smiled at me and gave me a chip and some dip, and now I think that means I can say hi to her at school. Maybe we'll sit by each other in class. Maybe I can hang with her and Josh and laugh when our car breaks down. Maybe that's what her smile and the chip and the dip mean. Maybe it's the start of a beautiful friendship.

CHAPTER SEVEN

I'm in," Josh declares.

"Wait—I'm supposed to convince you with all sorts of important and meaningful reasons about why I must do this. A quest unfulfilled, and all that."

"Whatever. You don't have to sell me. The open road. A far-off destination. I'm there."

Maybe it's good that was so easy. If Josh wasn't so enthusiastic, I might have caved and gone straight to Penny's parents' house to confess.

"But riddle me this: Why are we going to see Penny? Isn't she, like, the root of all stupidity at this point?"

"No, well, not really. She's just lost. And if we find her, then I've fulfilled my promise to her and myself that I won't tell anyone where she is. Then I'm going to make her turn herself in, tell her to grow a set, and finally rid my psyche of this hold she's had on me for the last year."

"Fair enough. So do we go home and pack? Or should we rough it?" Josh asks.

I'd hate to go back home and find the cops waiting outside my house. Or worse, run into my mom and have to lie or be guilted into confessing something. "Let's just go. We can buy some stuff along the way." Which really means Josh can use his dad's credit card and we can buy whatever we want. I never was one to take advantage of that as much as other people, although I rarely said no to a free meal. That would be rude, right? But this is the perfect—even noble—excuse to mooch. "But along the way where? Do we just head west and hope to find her standing on the side of the road?"

"West sounds best," Josh amuses himself. "Nobody ever found adventure by driving east. Or at least not in the movies."

"Which is practically real life anyways," I concur. "Our ultimate goal can be Portland because that's probably— maybe, anyways—where she might be. It's the biggest lead we have. And it certainly is west. About as far west as we can go, really. West to Portland!" I raise my pointer finger into the air in a declaration. Then Josh gets this *boing!* idea look on his face. "What's going on in that wacky head of yours?" I ask.

"Best idea ever," Josh declares. "*Hiding Out.*"

"Oh, no. No. No?" *Hiding Out* is this absurd movie from the eighties that always seems to be on the local crap channel at two in the morning. It stars Jon Cryer, the dad from *Two and a Half Men*, as someone who has to go into hiding for witnessing a murder or something, so he stops at a gas station, takes an ugly T-shirt off a rack, grabs a razor, bleach, and some shaving cream, heads to the bathroom and proceeds to shave off his beard and bleach his hair into the ugliest skunk do. Then he enrolls in high school. "Which part of *Hiding Out* are we talking exactly?" I'm leery. "Because I'm not going back to high school. Or shaving my beard."

"Let's buy ourselves wardrobes from Mars' Cheese Castle! And dye our hair in the bathroom!" Josh is hyperenthused, almost more than the time he found a copy of the ancient *Hitchhiker's Guide to the Galaxy* computer game on eBay. A little scary, really. But also kind of funny, too. I shrug an OK, and we head inside. At least it's the beginning of a plan.

On our way in, we pass the cop and the baseball-hat bitch-mom coming out. The cop nods at me, and I wink at her.

"Did you just wink at that cop?" Josh whispers.

"Yep," I answer. I just winked at a cop.

The Castle is buzzing with tourists sifting through fridges and freezers of cheese fare. We make our way over to the racks of Wisconsinalia clothing. Josh pulls out a green shirt that proclaims, WISCONSIN: SMELL OUR DAIRY AIR. I laugh and find a tank top reading, WISCONSIN: SMELLS LIKE CHEESE.

"Half of these are about smells," I note.

53

"And the other half are about cows."

"And the other half are about cheese *and* cows," I add.

We grab a selection of goofy shirts, some grotesque sport shorts, Packers boxers, bikini undies covered in cheese wedges for me, and a couple Badgers fleece blankets. In the grocery section we pack a Styrofoam cooler with pop, chips, CornNuts, beef jerky, bread and, of course, cheese. Josh adds a couple of cheese hats—giant yellow foam hats in the shape of cheese wedges—at the register. I give him a quizzical look. "In case we need a disguise," he says. As if wearing wedges of yellow Swiss on our heads will make us incognito. The hair dye will have to come later, since that is one product that Mars' Cheese Castle does not carry. If only it were cheese based.

Whenever I imagined a no-holds-barred shopping spree, à la *Pretty Woman*, I thought it would be in a fancy department store, complete with doting salesgirls and an appropriate montage soundtrack. Never did it involve cheese products.

We pack up the car and are about to drive away when I realize, "Wait. We don't have any maps."

"Maps? We don't need no stinkin' maps," Josh accents.

"Right. We already barely have any idea where we're going, but we're going to try and get there without maps? I don't think so."

"All we have to do is drive west, baby." Josh has one

hand on the steering wheel, one hand hanging next to me on my seat back.

"Yeah, and end up fried to a crisp in Death Valley. I'll be right back."

"You have a morbid imagination!" Josh yells after me as I walk into the Cheese Castle.

I pick out a few maps in the Castle, add in a pack of Chuckles, and then we're off.

"So which way do we go?" Josh asks.

I pull out the Wisconsin map and scan westward. Portland is a long way off, so we have a lot of possible terrain to cover before we either (a) find Penny or (b) give up and turn her in. As long as we're on the road, we may as well stop and see some of our glorious country before I go off to school (or get thrown in jail for aiding a fraud) and Josh goes, well, somewhere. I trace my finger along the treasure of lines and spot something that jars a wonderful family (pre-divorce devastation) road-trip memory. "The House on the Rock!" I yell. "We have to go!" I'm so excited I'm bouncing in my seat.

"What's the House on the Rock?" Josh asks, intrigued.

"Words do not describe, my dear. Just drive where I tell you."

"Aye aye, Captain."

"I can't hear you . . . ," I sing.

"Aye aye, Captain!" Josh cries, and we drive off singing the *SpongeBob* theme song.

About an hour into the two-hour drive to House on the Rock, I remember I told my mom that I'd call the police back. Basking in the state of Wisconsin masked but didn't rub out the whole point of this impromptu journey: Penny the kidnapee.

"I have to call the police." I turn down the stereo and yell over the open windows, "To tell them I don't know anything."

"Lying to the cops. Nice!" Josh enthuses. I doubt he'd be that way if he was the one doing the calling. Actually, he probably would.

"I need to center myself. Get my lie face on." I close my eyes and try to remember why I'm covering for Penny in the first place. Hummer. Babysitter. Olive tree. I feel a *pluff* on top of my head, and I look up to see that Josh has installed the cheese hat on me.

"Your disguise," he informs me.

"Naturally," I agree. "Roll up your window so I can hear." Josh uses the hand crank on the aged Eurosport door to muffle the highway noise, and I clear my throat. I beep through my phone to find the cop's number, then will myself to hit Send.

"Sergeant Sundstrom." His serious voice answers after one ring.

"Yeah, hi, this is Lillian Erlich. You left me a message. . . ."

"Right, yes. We're looking for Penny Nelson. We

believe her to be missing. You were the last person she spoke to. Did she say anything about going out? Meeting up with someone? Leaving town?" His questions sound slightly accusatory, as if he knows I know something. Is there some heat reader that can sense my guilt through the phone? I grip the cheese hat for strength.

"No, sorry, she didn't say anything. Is she going to be OK?" I fake distress, but it's difficult when Josh grabs my knee and busts up. I shoot him a shut-up look, and he takes his hand off my knee to put a shush finger to his lips.

"Well, what did she call you about at four thirty in the morning?" He clips as if calling someone at four thirty in the morning is something unheard of. Does he remember being eighteen? I argue with him in my head, convincing myself I'm completely in the right.

"Just, you know, to talk. About her night. Her boy-friend."

"What can you tell me about her boyfriend?" Is this a trick question? Am I somehow going to drag Gavin into this? Should I? Wouldn't be so bad for the cops to put a little scare into him. Why not.

"Well, truthfully, officer, he's kind of a dick. Pardon my French. Cheats on her. Says nasty things to her. Maybe worse. Hard to say. She doesn't tell me everything." There's a pause, and I can hear him scribbling everything down. "Look, I kind of have to go because I'm driving and shouldn't really be talking on the phone for safety reasons, but if you hear anything, please keep me posted. I'm really worried."

"Sure thing, miss. I'll be sure to call you if I need to talk to you." Again with the tone. We hang up.

Josh claps admirably. "Well done, Cheesehead." I pull the sponge hat off and toss it into the backseat. Josh and I roll our windows down, and the loud music resumes.

That wasn't so hard. Lying to the police. It almost helped suppress the guilt I'm sort of feeling about not telling Penny's parents. Maybe I should wear a cheese hat more often.

CHAPTER EIGHT

We drive up the winding gravel road that leads to the House on the Rock around three in the afternoon.

"What the hell is this place?" marvels Josh as we walk toward the building.

You wouldn't know it from the approach, but the House on the Rock is a glorious, never-ending collection of FREAK. I have only been here once before, when my extended family stopped during a fishing trip to Minnesota. Its grandiose grotesqueness awed me then, and I hope it doesn't disappoint now that I'm older.

The admission desk has a small line, and when we get up to the teller, a sallow teen with leftover acne, she drones, "Welcome to the House on the Rock."

"Tough day?" Josh kibitzes, and the charm oozes a smile right out of House on the Rock girl.

"Oh, you know, tourists." She rolls her eyes.

"Yeah, tourists." Josh chuckles as though we're House

on the Rock neighbors and we're just stopping by on our way to Sam's Club.

"So, would you like Tour One, Tour Two, Tour Three, or the Ultimate Experience?" she asks Josh, me being invisible, and all.

Josh turns to me and asks, "Do we want Tour One, Tour Two, Tour Three, or the Ultimate Experience?" in a mocking tone that's only obvious to me.

"I always want the ultimate experience, Josh," I say in an overtly sexual way. The girl at the counter looks surprised to see me there, and then pretends to shuffle some papers. Well, she doesn't pretend to shuffle, but I'm pretty certain those papers didn't need to be shuffled.

"We'll take two for the Ultimate Experience," Josh says and hands over the credit card.

To truly appreciate the House on the Rock, one must experience the mishegoss for themselves. But I'll try to do it justice.

We enter the first part, the House, which is an ultimate experience in itself. The story goes that some guy, Alex Jordan, found a fancy rock formation and decided he'd like to build a house around it. But not just any house. The House on the Rock has a groovalicious midget feel to it. The entire place is coated in shag carpeting, including several walls, and the ceilings were not meant for humans of my or Josh's stature. All of the weirdly winding nook-and-cranny rooms (complete with in-ground tiny round bed) lead up to the pinnacle and name inspiration for this place, a very long, narrow glass room—we're talking twenty-five feet, maybe fifty (I didn't bring my tape measure)—that juts out over the rocky nature below. The "room" ends in a tiny point, where you can look down through a small square window and see some trees. The fear factor is that the room bounces as you walk in it because it is so precariously out there. Josh makes it a point to freak out nearby small children for a good ten minutes by standing in the long room and saying things like, "Did you hear a crack? Is this thing sound?" and "I definitely felt us get lower. We should get out of here!"

I finally manage to drag him to the next segment of our Ultimate Experience when a little freckled redhead starts to cry. Once we make it through the cramped house, the place opens up into this massive compound of bizarreness. Rooms filled with giant calliope music-box things (that play themselves if you feed them money), a huge room with a giant whale blaring the Beatles' "Octopus's Garden" and other nautical nonsense, and the greatest, yet grossest, of all sights, a room filled with an enormous carousel. This is not a carousel one rides, however, but one you must watch, in horror, as it rotates in garish decadence. I need a thesaurus to find as many words as required to describe the monstrosity of the House on the Rock carousel. Everything here at the House on the Rock is BIG (except, of course, for the miniatures, of which there are many, including an entire circus re-created in tiny painted clowns).

"What the frig . . . ?" Josh can't even complete his sentence, he's so struck by this lewd creation. One might be able to get past the thirty zillion Christmas lights (in June) strung about, or the paint chipping off the numerous mystical beasts attached to the double-decker carousel's poles. But no one can ignore the tasteless "angels" floating above. "Are those mannequins?" Josh asks, incredulous.

"Why, yes, Josh," I answer as the House on the Rock authority. "Yes, they are." And they are. Above the carousel hang dozens of underdressed store mannequins, suspended by obvious wires, wearing trashy wigs and all looking kind of slutty.

"This place rocks!" Josh proclaims. "House on the Rock pun intended."

Two hours, one very large funnel cake, and way too many quarters spent on calliope music later, we've made it through the House on the Rock. Josh and I rest on a glossy log bench, when my cell phone slips out of my pocket and clatters to the floor.

"Freakin' phone," I declare. "I bet road trips were so much cooler before people could find you whenever they wanted."

"That's why I don't have a cell phone. If I want people to find me, I'll let them find me. Cell phones are like tracking devices. And if I need to know the time, I'll just ask someone. Why don't we just get rid of it," Josh suggests. "Toss it out the window in the long H-O-R room, over the rocks of H-O-R." We have officially shortened House on the Rock to the shorter and funnier HOR.

"I don't think I'm ready for that kind of freedom." I shake my head. "What if my mom calls?" My mom! I haven't yet told her about the impromptu road trip. She should be OK with it, since I already took a short road trip over spring break with Josh and some friends to the Wisconsin Dells. But just to be safe, I call her before we leave the HOR and explain, "Josh has commandeered me, Mom, to take me on one last road trip before I leave him and go away to college." She laughs, knowing full well that she can trust Josh (to keep his hands to himself, sadly, plus the financial aspect of the whole thing). She's a pretty great mom as far as moms go; she gave me a card a few months ago for my eighteenth birthday telling me that I'm finally free but to stop by for coffee and a hug every once in a while. It was her mom way of telling me that I'm an adult who still has a mommy. I love her so much for that.

"Just keep me posted on how you're doing. I suppose this can be your substitution for backpacking across Europe?" she asks, hopeful. Mom always used to talk about *her* backpacking trip before she went off to college, which sounded amazing to me. But, really, I couldn't ever be bothered to sit down and plan something like that. Mom doesn't know that, though, so—voilà!—perfect excuse for this trip instead.

"Do you want to call your dad?" I offer the phone to Josh.

"I don't want to waste the batteries. Besides, what's the point? He probably won't even notice I'm gone. If he comes home at all while we're away." The mood is darkened just a bit, so I don't press it. He probably wouldn't share much more even if I did.

Josh and I hang out in the HOR entrance, looking over the plentiful pamphlet displays for nearby tourist attractions. When I was a kid, I used to collect the pamphlets, plucking out ones that looked interesting and might be worth visiting someday, when I was grown-up enough to make those kinds of decisions. I'd gather pamphlets of natural formations, water shows, outlet malls, and doll museums. Most of them ended up on the floor of our car to dissolve under the muck of winter boots.

We decide to spend the night somewhere nearby, so we can head out early the next morning. Scanning the lodging section, I spot the hilariously named "Don Q Inn." "Like *Don Quixote*?" I ask, referring to the wacked-out movie (based on a book, of course) we watched in Spanish class, which inspired my Spanish class name, Dulcinea. Even better, the Don Q Inn is a FantaSuite Hotel in a nearby town.

"FantaSuite?!" Josh and I yell in unison, and I note a couple of grannies glaring at us from a table cut from a great redwood tree. "Sorry." I shrug at them. Don't want to upset the grannies.

The Don Q Inn is one of those hotels in which each room has its own theme. " 'Let our FantaSuite suites transport you to the world of your dreams. Each is a unique experience, an adventure, a romantic retreat designed to completely immerse you in the getaway of your choice,' " Josh reads.

"I want to be immersed!" I yell, too excited at the doofosity to contain myself. We proceed to read the room themes to each other: Arabian Nights (Aladdin!), the Blue Room (complete with three-hundred-gallon copper cheese vat tub!), Casino Royale (Vegas!), the Cave (Caveman!), the Float (a Viking ship!), Indian Summer (a wigwam!), Mid-Evil (a poorly spelled room with shackles on the bed!), Northern Lights (full-size igloo!), the Swinger (a hanging bed!), and Shotgun (hunting theme!). Josh and I both zero in on one, and we don't even have to ask.

"Tranquility Base, baby. That's where we're headed," Josh informs me.

"You took the spacey words right out of my mouth." The room choice is a no-brainer: a re-creation of a Gemini space capsule, complete with moon crater whirlpool. "But wait. Wasn't Tranquility Base part of the Apollo 11 mission?"

"I suppose," Josh muses.

"So wouldn't that make this suite historically inaccurate?"

"Right. They're very concerned with historical accuracy at the Don Q Inn. That's why they plopped a heart-shaped bed in the middle of a cave."

"You never know. That could be historically accurate. I have heard of cave paintings with heart-shaped beds in them. Right next to the wooly mammoth wearing a Snuggie." Josh smiles at me out of the corner of his eye.

The buzz of HOR and the prospect of Tranquility Base are enough to get any human jazzed, but in the back of my mind (OK, more like really close to the front) is the fact that Josh and I are going to be staying in a hotel room together. Alone. With a whirlpool and a round bed. The Penny Quest has just taken a very interesting turn, and I'm not talking about the one aiming us at Portland.

• • •

My mom gave me a birthday gift today. A week and a half early. She said she couldn't wait. Couldn't even wait to wrap it, so she didn't. The box was from QVC. I had a million guesses based on recent shows I caught her watching. Was it from Joan Rivers's collection? Quacker Factory? Iman Global Chic? But no. None of the above. Not even anything I saw her watching. She really surprised me this year. An olive tree. Because I once asked for an olive off her salad plate. I guess that's thoughtful. But where will I put it?

CHAPTER NINE

Let me back up to the History of Me and Josh to explain the platonicity of the situation.

It all started freshman year, study hall (as most things do). Josh had on these insanely huge, chain-bedraggled purple pants, and I had on these really skinny jeans, also in purple. We ended up alphabetically next to each other (yes, they gave us assigned seating in study hall so that they could easily spot the ditchers by the holes in the grid). Josh leaned over my desk and asked, "Excuse me. Do you have a purple pen I could borrow?" Hilarious, right? Turned out he had some friends who were dating some of my friends they met at DQ while I was away being a junior counselor at overnight camp. At the time he was dating a friend of a friend (the first in a long list of dullards who never interested me, or him, enough to make much of an impression). We started as friends, so I guess we just kind of *continued* that way. I think guys—some, maybe most, but hopefully not all—are incapable of liking girls in a girlfriend way if they like them in a friend way first. Because Josh has never even attempted to be physical with me beyond hugging (nonsexual), kissing (on the cheek or forehead), or smacking my butt (football player manner). He still sometimes says things in flirty ways (using names like *sweetheart, baby, cutie*), but I think that's more out of habit than due to the fact that I could possibly be an attractive female if he'd just screw in his eyeballs correctly. I just grossed myself out.

I, on the other eyeball, have had a crush on him from purple day one. Since before we met, actually, when I saw him play guitar at Lizzy Rubin's junior high graduation party. I'm such a sucker for guys in bands, even more of a sucker when it comes to guitarists who also sing harmony parts (So supportive! Yet, what do we really know about them?). I'm very good at playing it cool around guys (which probably accounts for the very small, count them on one hand, not every finger, number of boyfriends I've had in my life), which makes me, well, very cool to have as a girl friend.

Fast-forward to the end of senior year, exactly four weeks before prom. I'm embarrassed, ashamed, hitting-myself-in-the-head pathetic because I wanted, no *needed*, to go to the prom. Who can explain why? Was it all the movies and TV shows and books that glorify the crap out of this ritual? Did I really believe that I'd be the girl, so common and blendy until my glorious, glam debut in some budget hotel's ballroom that everyone would whisper, "Who's that?" "Don't you know? That's Lillian Erlich." "But she's so beautiful . . ." And then Josh would swoop in, my date in powder blue, and say, "I didn't need a prom dress to tell me how hot you are," and he'd grab me, dip me, and kiss me passionately while balloons and sparkles fell from the ceiling and the whole room applauded.

Not how it happened. Four weeks before prom, neither Josh nor I had dates. Josh could not have cared less, but I had a countdown in my head that said if no one asked either of us by four weeks prior to prom, I would ask Josh. As a friend. So I did. And he answered, "Why not?" Six hours of dress shopping later, I was ready for my close-up in, what else, a skimpy little purple dress. Only one week later, I got a call from Josh.

"Yeah. About prom . . . ," he started.

Of course like a douche I had to interrupt with "Do you think we should try to match? Like in a kind of funny way? But so we look good in pictures? Or is that stupid? Or is that funny stupid? Do I have to get you a corsage? What do you call a guy corsage? A boutonniere?"

"Lil." Josh caught a break between my pathetic desperations and said, "Look, I've been thinking. This is our senior prom and all, and maybe I want to go with, you know, someone I like more than a friend?" No response from me except in my stomach, which initially jumped up to my lungs but quickly plummeted to near bathroom floor horror. "I kind of just asked Liza Bell."

I know, I know. It makes him sound like the biggest prick when I tell that story, but when I put myself in his shoes, I mean, *I* wanted to go with someone I liked more than a friend.

I ended up spending prom night on the couch, watching prom-themed horror movies (*Carrie, Prom Night, Prom Night 2*) with several boxes of stale Girl Scout Cookies I found in the pantry and a bottomless bowl of popcorn I whipped up in the Whirley Pop. Not exactly a memory for the keepsake book.

Tonight, now, it's just us. No boyfriends. No girlfriends. No external crushes who may sneak their way into the lunar module. One bed—one round, somewhat hysterical, space-themed bed. And the two of us. Heading west. However we get there.

CHAPTER TEN

We need to pick some stuff up at the drugstore," Josh says through bites of Pizza Hut thin-crust cheese-and-pineapple pizza. There are very few food options near the Don Q, and we wanted something quick, easy, and familiar. We called the Don Q to reserve Tranquility Base and were pleasantly surprised to find it available at such short notice. Maybe it's more popular during seasons of high space travel.

I pick out my salad from the salad bar, which I got because I always pretend I'm going to try and eat a little healthy on a road trip, when, really, what's the point? It's a road trip. But more important—what does Josh need at the drugstore?

When someone says they need to stop at the drugstore, particularly someone who will be staying at a hotel later in the evening, the first thing I assume is condoms. Does that make me a perv? Or just hopeful?

After picking out lettuce, tomatoes, croutons, and

Thousand Island dressing, I return to the table with my response. "So what do you need at the drugstore?" Casual, real casual.

"Well, seeing as we didn't plan on a road trip, we'll need to get toothbrushes and multivitamins, stuff like that."

"Naturally." I nod.

"And what else, Lil?" He's prodding me to answer for him, to anticipate his thoughts and needs.

I would hate to be wrong on this one. Mortified to be wrong. So I just say, "I give up."

Josh sighs. "*Hiding Out*, dude. The hair dye? We still haven't done our hair, Cryer style."

"Right. Hair dye. Of course." Remind me to hit my head against a wall later.

At Walgreens we scan the shelves of hair dye. I don't know how anyone chooses between walnut brown and espresso brown and hazelnut brown, except by what they might want to eat.

Josh saunters over to me with a box, holding it near his face as if straight out of a commercial. "What do you think?" He glances shiftily at the box. "Is it me?" I read the box, "Sunshine Blonde," complete with bouncy-headed babe on the cover.

"Looks just like you," I say. "Except she has blue eyes."

"So who are you going to be?" he asks. "How about we do a *Legend of Billie Jean* on you?" *The Legend of Billie*

73

Jean is yet another late-night TV movie of the eighties, about some small-town Southern folk who get themselves mixed up with the law after a lecherous old guy gropes the main character (Billie Jean), and something involving her little brother's bike. A little too complicated for my late-night lucidity. The most memorable part of the movie is when Billie Jean cuts off her long, blond hair into this tough short cut and gets all badass. She keeps shouting, "Fair is fair!" My other favorite part of the movie is when this other character thinks she got shot, but really she just got her period for the first time. They just don't make movies like that anymore.

"I never said I'd *cut* my hair," I argue. "I need enough for a summer ponytail." I scan the shelves for a color that I like. It's hard to look past the absurdly posing faces on the boxes to imagine what the hair color would look like on my head.

"How about this?" Josh walks up behind me, leans his head on my shoulder, and wraps one arm around me with the box in his hand. "You know I like your hair red," he says in a way I want to describe as purring, but that would imply something. The color is called "Copper Rust," which I think might technically be a shade of green. I take the box from his hand and walk over to a small mirror in the beauty aisle. Holding the box next to my face, I squint to try and imagine what it would look like translated onto my head. I don't know if it's really me. I've kind of always wanted to dye my hair dark, add a little brooding mystery to my look. Red hair doesn't seem very brooding, and how can I be mysterious if my tall red head stands above a crowd? But, Josh . . .

"OK." I sigh with acceptance.

We pick up loads of other toiletries and snacks, as well as a local newspaper so I can read the comics and Dear Abby. I scan the last-minute-impulse buys while Josh spills the contents of our tiny shopping basket onto the less-than-ample counter. Thanks, Josh's dad.

We pull up to the Don Q Inn, an unassuming, almost barnlike building that I half expected to look like a castle. Strike two on the castle front. There are only four other cars in the parking lot. Maybe Sundays aren't the busiest nights. I'm picturing kinky couples on weekends and discreet affairs on weeknights. Sundays are sacred after all. So I've heard.

Standing behind the desk is a vulture-bald man wearing a mustard yellow suit jacket, red tie, and white shirt. He stares ahead, not at us, not at a TV, or even a wall, but in that locked stare that means your body may be present but your mind is somewhere else. Maybe he's picturing himself in one of the suites, I'm thinking Mid-Evil, with a saucy wench.

A hotel bell is perched on the desk in front of Mustard Man, and even though by this time the man has unenthusiastically noticed us (his eyes now look at, not through, me), Josh finds the need to ding the bell.

"Yes?" Mustard Man breathes.

"Hello. We have a reservation for Tranquility Base. Under Erdman," Josh says formally.

Mustard Man lets his index finger fall onto his keyboard. Tap. Pause. Tap. Pause. I take a long look around the lobby as I wait for Mustard Man to finish his turtle typing. There's a rustic charm to this place, if you enjoy wood paneling, wagon wheels, and hideous patterned carpeting. The theme is hodgepodge, by the looks of the flowered sofas, brick walls, and multiple television sets. The centerpiece of the room is a large, round, metal fireplace, complete with midsummer fire, and surrounded by what are either old-fashioned dentist chairs or old-fashioned barbershop chairs, but I don't know which since I'm not old-fashioned. Whatever they are, they all come in a variety of pleather colors, sure to delight any dental or barber patron.

Mustard Man scares me when he says too loudly for being so close to him, and, well, being one of only two people in the entire grand room, "You want Tranquility Base. That's one of our deluxe suites, which goes for a hundred seventy-four a night." He looks at us dumbly.

"We just need one night," Josh tells him while he pulls out the old man's credit card.

"But of course you do," Mustard Man replies without

76

affect. "I'll just need to see proof of age." He points with his handy, all-purpose index finger to a sign that reads, TWO ADULTS, 18 AND OVER IN SUITES ONLY. I dig into my purse, really just an old canvas bag I bought with a picture of vintage Pinocchio on it, and fish out my driver's license. Mustard Man nods after thorough inspection of both IDs, and proceeds to tap on his keyboard. Still tapping, he tells us, "Indoor pool is down the hall. Outdoor pool is outside. Local calls are free, as is the continental breakfast. Checkout is noon. Your room comes with a hot tub, and there are extra towels in your suite. Call housekeeping if you need more. Just down that hall to the left." His lips strain out a millisecond smile, and he hands us a key card.

"Just curious," I ask Mustard Man. "What other rooms are people staying in tonight?"

"I'm sorry, ma'am, I cannot divulge that information." He's serious about enforcing whatever hint of power he has here. I'm guessing he's just too lazy to look them up.

"Well, thank you anyway," Josh says jovially, and we head off to Tranquility Base.

There's definitely suspense as the key card enters the slot. The light flashes green, click, and we're in.

"Noooo way," Josh exhales. He's right. No way does this place exist anywhere but in some basement dweller's sick imagination. The walls are faux moon, craggy and gray, alternating with dark blue walls covered in planets of various sizes and colors. To the right of the door is a regular old hall closet (just like in outer space!), and to the left is a regular old bathroom. I walk farther in and spy the hot tub, center stage, fully tiled and surrounded by moon rock. Above it and around it stands a lunar module. Maybe it would look authentic (umm, authentic hot tub on the moon?) were it not for the twenty-inch television next to the average leather chair next to the window air conditioner. A not-at-all-spacey lamp sits on a table with a less-than-futuristic hotel telephone.

"I do not feel as though I am in space," I disappointedly tell Josh.

"Maybe it's not supposed to feel like we're *in* space, just that we're pretending like we think we're in space? But more important, how many people do you think have done it in that whirlpool?" Josh asks, sounding both disgusted and intrigued.

"I hope they have a thorough housekeeping staff. What if it's just Mustard Man and his index finger?" I shake my head at the thought.

We're exploring the room, when I note, "There's no bed." Then Josh discovers some gloriously snot green carpeted steps hidden among the crags of the moon. "Lead the way," I command, and I follow him up the narrow, winding stairway to the top of the lunar module that we saw from below.

"The bed is the lunar module!" Josh exclaims. "Oh, man. Too cool." He dives onto the bed and lays on his side. "There's a TV in the walls of the bed! And check this out." He runs his hand along the pillows lining the inside of the module. "Vellllllvet." He draws the word out in a velvety way. I sit down on the bed and look around at the space paintings on the walls. "Where do you think they find round sheets to fit the round bed?" Josh asks.

"Probably just use regular sheets and tuck them in, I'm guessing."

"Don't ruin the mystique." He flips around the channels of our in-bed TV. I scooch in so I can see the small screen, and so I can be closer to him on the bed. I'm assuming we'll sleep together tonight, since there's only one bed. And by that I mean snooze-type sleeping together, not the other kind. Josh obviously has no interest in the other kind as he settles in with an episode of *South Park* and guffaws at the TV.

"I'm gonna go dye my hair," I decide. I want there to be a note of spite in my voice, like, if you ignore me maybe I *will* go away, but Josh doesn't detect it.

"OK. I'll do mine when you're done."

I head downstairs to the bathroom and follow the directions on the package. While I let the color sink in, I decide to run the hot tub. Just to see. Josh hears the jets and calls down, "What are you doing? I can't hear the TV!"

"I'm filling the hot tub. Might as well get our money's worth," I yell.

"I'll be down after this episode."

The glow of the digital clock, another not-exactly-spacey detail, helps me time my hair color as I slip out of my socks and shorts. I unhook my bra through the back of my T-shirt and wriggle the shoulder straps over each arm, then out the holes of the sleeves. The tub is almost full now, so I set one foot in gingerly to acclimate the rest of my body, then the other. I sit down in the hot, foamy water, experiencing the weird sensation of being in a hot tub wearing cotton underwear. The water hits only halfway up my T-shirt, weighing the rest of it down. I stretch my legs out and touch the bubbly jets with my toes. Using my big toe as a stopper, I plug the flow of bubbles, then open it. Plug. Unplug. I close my eyes for a few minutes, recalling the drama of the day.

It all started with "*I did it.*" And she did do it—I'll give her that. But who *does* that? I remember being little and planning elaborate runaway scenarios when I was mad at my parents, going so far as to pack a bag with only the most essential items—my blankey, my Snoopy nightgown, a copy of *The BFG*, and a roll of Life Savers (in case I choked, I could breathe through the hole until it melted).

Faking your own kidnapping seems like so much trouble to go through to get away.

I almost drift off to sleep when I hear Josh clomping

down the green stairs. My eyes open and adjust to read the time on the digital clock. My hair! I jump up out of the hot tub, wring out the butt on my shirt, and grab a nearby towel to wrap around my waist like a skirt. The bathroom has a tub-shower combo, so I turn on the tub spout until the water is nice and warm. On my knees, I flip my head forward under the faucet and watch as the Copper Rust showers from my hair down the drain. When the water begins to run clear, I sit up, grab a towel, and dry off. I toss the towel on the floor and see I have stained it with orange blotches. Will they charge us for that? Or will they think it's some menstrual mess and just bleach the crap out of it and pass it along to the next unassuming FantaSuiter?

My hair looks darker than expected, although I definitely see the brightness of red underneath the dusky, wet strands. I pull the hair dryer from its resting place on the bathroom wall and dry my hair until I can see the true color. It's quite pretty, actually, shiny and fiery. It could almost look natural if it weren't for the dye stains around my forehead and on my ears.

"Ta da!" I walk out of the bathroom for my hair debut. Josh is in the hot tub, shirtless in his boxers.

"Rrreddd," he drawls. "Lookin' good."

I walk over to the tub, feeling brazen with my new look, and drop my skirt towel on the floor so that my undies show. I step into the hot tub and slither down next to Josh, not touching, but close. He slides away, just the slightest bit, to get a better look at my hair. "Now no one will recognize you," he says.

I so want him to look at me like I see him look at other girls. *Real* girls to him. But he pops up out of the water and says, "My turn," then drips water all over me as he makes his way out of the tub and into the bathroom.

I extend my legs, plug the bubble holes with my toes, and hang out, alone, in Tranquility Base. As tranquil as the name suggests.

Annabelle hates me. That's what she told me. She watched me get ready for Gavin, put on the bra that he likes best with the brown and red lace, and the flowy but fitted wrap dress with the red roses on it. It usually almost makes me feel beautiful when Annabelle watches me, like she maybe wants to be me. I imagine her thinking about when she gets older and has a boyfriend who loves her like Gavin loves me. But when I told her that she had to stay in her room because Gavin was coming over and he wanted to be alone with me, just me, and all we have is one hour until Mom and Dad get home, and I wanted to be alone with him so bad. . . . She said she hates me. She said that Mom would be mad and ground me when she gets home from her gong yoga session. I said I'm already grounded all the time so what does it matter. That Gavin and I only get to see each other when I'm not bratsitting and he's not too busy for me. That school doesn't count, because we're not alone. Not like we could be if she would just do what I wanted for once. She said I suck and I'm the worst sister and Jenny Blick has a pretty sister who buys her presents and sings her songs and lets her stay up late to watch dirty movies. That's what good sisters do. And I said good sisters don't get everything they want and whine and tattle and say they hate you. Good sisters don't expect me to drive them everywhere without saying thank you. Good sisters look up to their big sisters for real. Then I locked her door and told her I'd give her twenty dollars and my favorite cashmere sweater if she'd just shut up until Gavin left, which wouldn't be very long anyway because Dad gets home from work soon and Mom will be back right after that. She said she would. And that she hates me.

CHAPTER ELEVEN

I'd love to be able to share the sordid details of our night together, but, alas, there are no sordid details to share. When Josh finally emerged from the bathroom, not as a blond but as a sort of sweet potato–flavored, I mean *colored,* mess (the bleach wasn't enough for his brown hair), I was already a shriveled prune danish and decided to get out of the tub and into bed. Josh, on the other hand, was all ready to chillax in the hot tub, and so by the time he came up to our round space bed of love, I was, as he told me seventy-six times and counting this morning, snoring like a silverback gorilla.

I dress in one of my new shirts, which reads, WISCONSIN: BEER, BRATS, AND CHEESE: THE BREAKFAST OF CHAMPIONS, and throw on a pair of cheese boxers as undies. We partake in the continental breakfast set out in the lobby—choice of three cereals from magical mechanical cereal dispensers in which all you do is turn a dial and *presto* the cereal dumps into your bowl, OJ, coffee, and assorted very dry, but still delicious enough pastries. It's only eight in the morning, but we decide to get on the road.

"One thing my dad always taught me"—flecks of cruller fly as Josh speaks from his green dentist-barber chair—"the early bird misses the traffic."

"Prophetic." I nod. I'm a tad peeved about last night because I guess I was expecting something to happen. But Josh doesn't have a clue. As usual.

After we stuff our faces to the point of feeling like continents (so that's why they call it a *continental* breakfast), I pull out a map of Wisconsin. We sit on a flowery couch in the lobby, having both exhausted ourselves of space-themed jokes ("That's one small crap for man, one giant turd for mankind," Josh proclaimed this morning as he emerged from the bathroom).

"We can either backtrack and head through Madison or take some smaller roads and hit I-Ninety at La Crosse," I tell Josh.

"No turning back," he states, ejecting himself from the green pleather.

"La Crosse it is."

Josh checks out, and I step into the hot Wisconsin summer. It's already humid, which means today will be sweaty in the Eurosport's lack of air-conditioning. I face the Don Q Inn and try to imagine who else is in there, doing what they're supposed to be doing in a FantaSuite theme room. What a waste.

When Josh emerges from the hotel in his dick shades and I CUT THE CHEESE IN WISCONSIN T-shirt, goofy smile displayed, I drop the spite and remember that we have plenty more hotels to come.

The car is already starting to look like a tornado hit indoors, so I tidy up by stuffing the maps into the glove box. But there's so much stuff already inside that the maps keep sliding out. Along with the maps, a photograph falls to the floor. "What's this?" I ask.

Josh peers over at me as he drives. "Oh. Um, that was from some party we were at. I thought it was a good picture, so I kept it."

It is a good picture. Me and Josh, with our arms around each other, vamping for the camera. My hair looks really good, edgily bobbed, and I have on my favorite perfectly fitted heather gray T-shirt. Josh looks even better. Model hot, but completely unaware of the hotness. I'm so drawn to this perfect couple that it takes me a minute to notice the figure in the background: Penny. She's holding a cup, shoulders tensed as they often are, and she's blatantly watching me and Josh. Her expression is hard to read. Is she happy? Intrigued? Jealous? Plotting to murder us in our sleep? Isn't there some detective trick whereby, in order to catch a killer, you have to get into their heads? Not that

Penny's a killer, but if she was? I don't know if anyone out there is smart enough to crack that code.

I put the photo in my wallet, just in case we need some sort of identifying picture of Penny along the way. That's what I tell myself, anyway. It's not just so I can look at me and Josh together. Why would I have to, since we're technically together now? If only we weren't so technical.

We stop for gas in La Crosse and marvel at the world's largest six-pack of beer (really giant beer vats painted to look like cans). I'm not sure if it's impressive or just slightly clever. How do we even know there's beer in there?

Outside of La Crosse and heading west we come upon an enormous bridge spanning a large body of water. A sign reads, MISSISSIPPI RIVER.

"Is this the Mississippi River?" Josh asks.

"That's what the sign says."

"The Mississippi River?" he asks again.

"Yes," I confirm.

"The M-I-S-S-I-S-S-I-P-P-I River?" Josh spells it out like we learned to do as kids.

"Why?" I ask, wondering what he's all bunged up about.

"Because this is like an iconic waterway. Mark Twain and all that. Huck Finn, you know?"

"Yeah. I guess." I shrug, trying to get into the spirit of road-tripping. "And we're like Huck and Jim? Only we're driving across the river, not paddling down it?"

"And I'm not black," Josh points out.

"And I'm not a boy. But I do have red hair," I point out.

"So it's really the same thing," Josh figures.

"I reckon."

We enter Minnesota with some fanfare, agreeing that we need a ritual every time we cross a new state line. Cheese hats on, we do a mini-wave (I raise my hands, then Josh does, long enough for the car to swerve slightly), we "Woo!" and then we yell, "Good-bye, Wisconsin, helllllooooooo, Minnesota!" Anything more elaborate and we'd probably forget by the time we get to the next state. Maybe we still will.

About two hours into Minnesota, I decide we need to change the music. Josh has been flipping the radio dial around the entire trip just to find obscure college radio from every town we pass through. Since my iPod is at home, and Josh's ancient car only has a tape deck anyway, our options are limited. "This is wrong," I decide. "This is not road-trip music."

"So what then?" he asks, annoyed that I dare usurp his unspoken rule that he always chooses the music.

"We'll find something else when we stop for lunch. Only ten minutes till Blue Earth." I have mapped out some stops along the way that don't look too small town (i.e., full of hillbilly serial killers waiting to drag me into a cornfield) or too big city (which always ends up in horrid highway complications and never quite lives up to our own big city, Chicago. Plus, big cities have no place in road trips). Blue Earth looks just about right, at least as far as I can tell by the dot on the map. Plus, it sounds sort of otherworldly.

Once we're off the highway, I insist that we top off our gas so we don't get stranded where we're not wanted (hillbillies in a cornfield, remember?). Josh fills the tank, and I explore the gas station for exotic Minnesotan snacks. Next to some Lurky Jerky, I spot a table filled with $1.99 cassette tapes. "Score," I say to myself. Most of the tapes belong to old and obsolete groups I've never heard of, but I manage to find a few oldies compilations and an Elvis Best Of. Driving along a highway just screams for old music, almost like we're driving backward into another time. I pay for the tapes and a Jumbo Gulp Dr. Pepper, and pick up a Minnesota scratch-off lottery ticket called Fishing for Franklins.

Josh is perched on the hood of the car, shirtless as ever, and leans on the windshield. I join him and ask him for a coin. "I want to scratch off this winning ticket," I tell him.

"Why'd you buy that? Those things are for suckers." He reaches into his pocket and pulls out a penny.

I rub off the silver flakes, one at a time to create some suspense, and end up with three matching number twelves. "What does this mean?" I scan the card for the rules, and figure out that I've just won twelve dollars. "Who's the sucker now?" I gloat. I head back inside the gas station to claim my reward and pick up some celebratory Slim Jims for later.

In the car, I pop in the new-old Elvis tape. Josh approves with a light nod, not wanting to give up his music monopoly just yet. "What is that?" He points ahead to some sort of huge sculpture just up the road. We drive toward it, and as we approach, we recognize the green man figure. It's the freakin' Jolly Green Giant.

"What the . . . ?" Josh leans forward to look up out the windshield at the statue. A message painted underneath the several-story-high statue (and I'm only guesstimating on the height, of course) reads, WELCOME TO THE VALLEY, BLUE EARTH, MN. We park and walk around the giant for a few minutes. "You think they make the vegetables here?" Josh asks.

I laugh. "*Make* the vegetables?"

"You know what I mean. Grow them?"

"Doubtful in Minnesota, with the winters and all. Can them maybe? Or perhaps this is the Jolly Green Giant's hometown."

Josh goes with it. "I wonder what it was like for him, growing up in Blue Earth. Must have been tough to find a winter coat."

"Or shoes," I interject.

"Was he always green? Always jolly? And did they really have to give him such a prominent junk lump?" We ponder these and other important questions until my cell phone rings and dances inside my pocket. I fish it out, and read the caller ID: a number I don't recognize from our home area code.

"Who is it?" Josh watches me as I stare at the phone.

"No clue. But it couldn't be Penny, could it? It's someone from home. And she's not home anymore. What if it's her dad calling from work or something? Or what if it's Gavin? Hell no, do I want to talk to him."

"But what if it's a clue! A lead! Answer it!" he commands. I don't want to. I think the Jolly Green Giant is trying to tell me through his ginormous leafy codpiece that I shouldn't answer. I let it go to voicemail.

"I'll just wait for the message," I tell him.

"Do what you gotta do. Even if it's not in the best interest of the mystery." I stick my tongue out at him like a pouty five-year-old. Josh ignores me. "We should hit the road," he says, and starts to make his way toward the Eurosport. "That Jolly Green groin is giving me the willies. Ha! The willies, get it?" I give a weak sympathy chuckle. On the way back to the car, I feel the buzz of voicemail and hesitantly push the button to listen. The giant's crotch had it right. This wasn't Penny.

"This message is for Lillian Erlich. This is Mike Lobel, FBI. We have reason to believe you may have some information on the whereabouts of Penny Nelson. Please call me at . . ."

I don't bother to write the phone number down. "Holy

turd stick," I say, and flip my phone closed with one hand. "That was the effin' FBI. They think I know something about Penny."

"Well, you do," Josh says all too matter-of-factly.

"How do they know that?" I'm bordering on hysterical.

"They're the FBI. *The Man*. Don't give it up to The Man, Lil."

"Give it up to The Man? What decade are you living in? And what do you care? You don't have to worry about them kicking you out of college before you even start and putting a big red *A* for *Accessory* on your record."

"Lil, we're out of high school. There's no more record."

"There's a police record! Which I may very well already have thanks to this dumbass runaway kidnapping faker. Damn." I'm so torn now just to tell them what I know. The FBI? That's kind of huge, right? But if they are the FBI, I mean, shouldn't they be able to figure things out for themselves? And, technically, I don't actually know where she is. I just know that at one point she told me she was maybe going to see some guy she knows in Portland. Or maybe I heard her wrong. After that, all she said was she did it, which really could have referred to anything that we had talked about after she may have mentioned a fake kidnapping plot. Maybe she bought that pair of Vans we had discussed. Or pierced her nose? She mentioned that once. How am I supposed to know what she did or didn't do? I'm not in the FBI. I'm just a recent high school graduate, out on the road with my best friend before I have to hunker down and go to college and study film or possibly creative writing. I don't even know what I'm going to major in, so how could I possibly know where my idiot friend is better than the FBI does? There it is. I don't know where Penny is, and therefore, I am not actually about to lie to the FBI.

"I'm calling the FBI guy back. Don't talk. Turn off Elvis." Josh clicks the radio and flashes me a stay-strong fist. I grab the cheese hat for support.

The phone only has to ring once before I hear, "Mike Lobel speaking." So serious.

"Uh, hi. This is Lillian Erlich? You called me?" Toughen up, Lil, you know *nothing*.

"Yes, Ms. Erlich. Recent developments have led us to believe that Ms. Nelson has not been kidnapped but has run away."

"Really? What developments?" I'm going for concerned friend, but I know I sound shifty.

"Several hundred dollars were withdrawn from Ms. Nelson's bank account two days prior to her disappearance. She was still residing at her family home when this occurred. We believe she used this money for a plane ticket. Since you are the last person she contacted before her disappearance, we are asking you to cooperate and give us any information you have about her whereabouts."

He is insinuating that I'm lying. I don't owe him any

information. If he could do his job right, if he could figure out that her parents don't give a crap where she goes or what she does as long as she's there for them when they need her services, maybe that'd give him some clues. Plus, isn't that what he gets paid for? "I'm sorry," I say, ever the concerned friend, "but I don't know where she is. Maybe you can ask her parents. Or her boyfriend, Gavin James. Check with him. I'm sure he'll have lots to tell you." That's right. Ask the guilty parties, not me. I didn't ask to be a part of this, and I didn't do anything wrong. Plain and simple.

"We are looking into connections with Gavin, but we think her communication with you is the key. We'd like to hear the voicemail she left you . . ."

"Yeeeeahhh, sorry. I deleted it. It was just late-night mumbling anyway, you know?"

"Well, we'll see if we can somehow retrieve it. Every clue helps."

"I'm sure it does," I say, with undetectable sarcasm.

"We'll be in touch." And Lobel hangs up.

"Turds ahoy. Can they check my erased voicemails?" I quickly call my voicemail and delete the Penny message.

"Not that I'm the authority on FBI technology, but I'm guessing yes. But don't worry about it, Lil. She didn't tell you anything really anyway, right?"

"True." I have convinced myself of this. "She didn't."

* * *

I almost went to the movie with Lillian and Josh and their friends. Our friends? I don't know if I can call them that. But that's OK. They were going to see a movie, a funny movie, one that made me laugh just by watching the commercial. Gavin elbowed me when I laughed at the commercial. What are you, retarded? he asked. That wasn't funny, he said. But it was. And he said he was busy tonight, so when Lillian called and asked, I said I could go. But I kept my phone with me just in case. In case he called. I didn't want it to ring, prayed it wouldn't, while I was in the theater. Because he would be mad. Other people might be, too, but it's him that matters. Luckily it rang before the movie started. I was buying popcorn, no extra butter, when the call came. He told me to come over. I almost told him I was busy. He asked where I was. I said I was at Target, buying some tampons for my mom. He said, She hasn't gone through menopause yet? Why would he want to know that? I said I'd be over as soon as possible. He said to be over even sooner. He can be romantic like that. Passionate. So of course I had to go. I told Lillian that I had really bad cramps and needed to go home. That's my standard excuse because who can argue against that? Or so I thought. Lillian was like, "Double-dose some Aleve and buy an extra-large bag of Sno-Caps. Mix them with the popcorn. That's the cramp

96

cure-all!" *I really did want to stay. That actually sounded tasty. And like I said, I wanted to see that movie. But Gavin was waiting. So I said, "Wish I could, but I always get diarrhea when I have my period." And then Josh was, like, "Thank you for that delightful splattering of information." He always says the right thing. The funny thing. Gavin wasn't in a funny mood when I picked him up. I almost told him the thing that Josh said about the diarrhea, but then I'd have to explain. Gavin and I spent the night hanging out in the car, sometimes driving, sometimes in the backseat, sometimes just sitting, me wondering what he was thinking. I kind of wish I could have seen the movie. Maybe I can rent it when it comes out on DVD. I'll just have to hide the box.*

CHAPTER TWELVE

The Elvis tape autoflips from side 1 to side 2 to side 1 again, and it fits the mood of our drive so nicely that we don't bother to switch tapes. I particularly love the song that starts all slick and slow: "She looks like an angel. Walks like an angel. Talks like an angel. But I got wise . . ." Pause pause. "You're the devil in disguise!" And it goes all jangly and out of control. I dub it my Penny song. Devil in disguise indeed. So what does that make me? A minion of some sort? I'm not crazy. I know I've been lying to myself. To everyone, really. Even as little as I listened to Penny that night before graduation, I heard her. And I remember. We were sitting at a booth at Copper Brothers Pancake House, one of those booths that's so big you can fit ten people in it but only two people can get out without crawling through the sticky mess underneath the table. I was trapped dead center, sandwiched in between Penny and Josh. Josh was in some heated discussion about the best brand of guitar strings with Nissa Bolger (or something along those same boring lines—lines I have heard one too many times that cause my eyes to glaze and my mind to wander), and whoever was on Penny's left, well, they made it clear that they were too enchanted with the other table half's conversation to turn their body toward Penny. So it was just us, alone at a giant tableful of people. Penny was talking ad nauseum about Gavin, her mom, her nonexistent fat issues. . . . I'd heard it all before, so I didn't try to hear it again. For a while I counted the number of distinct stained-glass lamps overhead, but I tired of that. So I interrupted her to ask about Ethan. I had been curious about him ever since she had come back a shade darker and a ginormous leap happier from her family's spring break trip to Disney World. Who was this guy who could do that to her? And why couldn't she remember that person instead of obsessing over Gavin, who made her face turn gray the instant he entered a room or called her on the phone? I asked her what Ethan was up to. Does she talk to him? Do they email? Is she going to see him again? And like I said before, she *shushed* me. All I could do after that was play with my fork and pray my apple pancakes arrived sooner rather than endless awkward minutes later. That's when she whispered, too quietly for a silent room, let alone a packed pancake restaurant table. The words I picked up— *Don't tell. Ethan. Portland. Leave.* I asked her to repeat. "You're going to visit Ethan in Portland and you don't want me to tell anyone?" I whispered it, I know, as quiet as a mouse, but there was the *shush* again. The suspiciously guilty glances around the room. Then, in her quiet manner, she eeked out, "I'm going to pretend I was kidnapped." And then the food came. The rush of the increased table volume. The shift of the conversations as the table shared food, summer plans. It all washed away her sentence. It's not as though she hasn't said weird things before. How many times has she threatened to run away or kill herself in some desperate grasp for attention? I was used to it. How was this different?

But it was.

Because she did it.

And as much as I want to pretend that I don't know where she is or how she got there, my subliminal pancake-loving mind didn't forget. Somehow the FBI knows I know. Which sucks. But why do they have to rely on me? Why don't her parents and her jagoff of a boyfriend know her well enough to know where she's going? Or that she even has to go anywhere? And then there's the whole road trip with Josh piece.

Penny was the perfect excuse to get Josh alone. Really alone, away from friends and parents and reality. Penny and her mindless mind made it possible for Josh and me to go on this trip. Not that we couldn't have without her as a destination, but neither of us have ever been motivated enough to plan something as huge as a cross-country road trip, no matter how unplanned it needed to be.

That's not exactly true.

I have plenty of motivation, hence going away to college in a few months. Hence working summer jobs. Hence having real, attainable goals. But Josh . . . his biggest motivation in life seems to be avoiding the unavoidable. Which he's really good at.

So a road trip together, before I become a new, improved college version of me, is my last chance. To figure out if we really are as perfect for each other as other people seem to think we are. As I have thought. Or hoped. I have Penny to thank for that. And all the guilt that's hiding inside of me—knowing how worried my mom would be if I ever pulled a stunt as mentally crap as Penny has pulled—is going to stay hidden until I get my perfect answer.

As if my mom reads my guilty mind, my phone buzzes, signaling a text. I flip it open. "How sit gong?" My mom's texting abilities are weak, but her message is crystal clear. I feel lucky she's thinking about me. I text her back with a smiley.

Josh and I do our best Elvis and sing along to the now overly familiar lyrics. I never realized how excellent Elvis's music is, too blinded by the sheer overexposure of his iconic self to realize there is an actual musician underneath to cause the hysteria. Maybe next road trip we can swing by Graceland. Will there be another road trip? Will there be another time of just me and Josh? What if he really does manage to gather a band and write good songs and go on tour? Or what if I get a summer job and don't have time for spontaneous travel? Or what if he gets a girlfriend? Or I actually find a guy I want to be with for more than a milli-second? So many what-ifs. This summer—this journey—is the only sure thing there is.

• • •

Last night was almost perfect. Close as my life can get, I suppose. Gavin was waiting for me by my locker, which can be a big deal. But he was in such a good mood. He scored something excellent or whatever from some guy, so he was sort of buzzed but so sweet I didn't mind. No one was home; Mom and Dad took Annabelle to a ballet on ice she wanted to see. Gavin and I watched TV on the big screen, the one we never get to use because my mom always bogarts it with her home shopping. Usually we only get to use the tiny one in my bedroom, which pisses Gavin off. It's like watching TV on someone's car DVD player through the back window of their minivan, he says. But not the huge, wall-covering flat screen. Would you believe my mom bought it on QVC? Yes. They even sell huge TVs. I guess so the fake gemstones look even bigger and more sparkly. How did they deliver it, though? Sorry I missed that.

We watched whatever channels Gavin flipped to randomly. He doesn't have the good cable at his house. I snuggled into him while he changed the channels and inhaled his after shave. He stopped on a cooking channel. The guy, who was from somewhere else, heavy with an accent, was making a shrimp pasta loaf thingy. It looked pretty gross. Shrimp are so ick, with their eyes and whiskers and tails. Gavin said to me, in between gulps of Code Red Mountain Dew, "Babe, I'm gonna make that for you someday." I'd eat it if he did. Googly shrimp eyes and all.

Then we kissed until my tongue fizzed with red pop.

CHAPTER THIRTEEN

Wind whips through the car as we drive in the right lane, the slow lane, on Interstate 90. Josh claims, "I'm just drivin' and in no hurry to get nowhere." I don't complain because the longer the trip takes, the farther away our destination of Penny is.

As soon as we enter South Dakota (insert New State Ritual here), we begin to see billboards for Wall Drug. Several read, WHERE THE HECK IS WALL DRUG? so I ask Josh, "*What* the heck is Wall Drug?"

"It's some sort of honkin' huge drugstore, I think. Loads of souvenir crap. My dad went there once on a 'business trip.'" Josh says this in air quotes with a wink. I have no idea what he's talking about, but I let it go. I don't ever feel the need to hear about his dad's rich bachelor lifestyle. "Supposed to be pretty wacky. We'll have to follow the signs to Wall."

I check the map and estimate, "We can make it there by tomorrow afternoon. Tonight we'll stay in Mitchell, home of the Mitchell Corn Palace." I didn't know what that was either, but if it's anything like the Mars' Cheese Castle, we're in for a lot of corn. And I do mean *corn*. Funny how both cheese and corn mean, well, cheesy and corny. Ah, the poetry of the road.

The car is too loud to really talk, so we pass the time with car games, like Slug Bug, I Spy, and counting vanity license plates. I decide to keep a record of the Wall Drug billboards, too, because they're pretty funny. Maybe they'll make their way into a story or film of mine someday. Some of the best:

WALL DRUG: NEW BACKYARD!

HAVE YOU DUG WALL DRUG?

NEW T-REX: WALL DRUG

HOT COFFEE ONLY 5 CENTS!

And about a million that declare, FREE ICE WATER.

"Can't you get free ice water pretty much anywhere?" Josh asks.

"Maybe there's something special about this water. Like, maybe it's not water at all but some brainwashing concoction that convinces you to buy tons of useless crap."

"Or maybe," Josh pontificates, "it's saliva from the new T. rex."

"Possibly, possibly. Or maybe it's actually pee from a garden gnome," I suggest.

"Pee from a garden gnome?"

"Yeah. From their new backyard."

"Where do you come up with this stuff?"

"I'm just brilliant, I guess." I fluff underneath my hair for emphasis.

"Beauty and brains." Josh shakes his head.

Don't let it fool you, I tell myself. He says that kind of stuff to anyone. Waitresses. Traffic cops. Circus clowns.

The exit for Mitchell appears right around dinnertime, and we follow the signs to head right to the Corn Palace. The air is sizzling; waving heat blurs mock our lack of air-conditioning.

"I could use some of that free ice water," Josh says as we find a parking space near the downtown.

I peel my thighs off the car seat fabric (grateful it's not leather) and step into Mitchell. The Eurosport is parked on a side street from the town's main street, free parking, and we head for the main thoroughfare (in a town like this, it's gotta be a thoroughfare) around a bunch of shops. Kitschy and creepy fabric humans—Native Americans and old men—sit on benches, ripe for photo ops. Josh poses with the stuffed people, kissing an old man's cheek, giving a Native American guy bunny ears, and I take a few pictures with my cell phone.

The instant we turn onto the main street, we can see the Corn Palace. This is no Mars' Cheese Castle. From a distance, it really does look like a palace, like the home of a sultan. As we get closer, we pass a street full of tourist shops, an ice cream parlor, and a doll museum shaped like a castle. So many tourist attractions, so many castles. "The Enchanted World Doll Museum!" I squeak. "We have to see it!"

"I don't know, man. Dolls. Kind of scary."

"Wuss," I say. "We're going after we visit the Corn Palace. Deal with it." I love old dolls. My mom has a collection from when she was little, but instead of coveting and hiding it, she let me play with the dolls. The old ones are the best, the way their eyes open and shut, their arms separated and poseable. They just seem more alive. In a good way.

Josh looks skeptical, so I grab his hand to let him know I'll comfort him through the terror. We walk down the street like this, holding hands, checking out the sights of Mitchell. Your casual observer might even think we're a couple. I catch our reflection in a store window, two tall faux redheads, holding hands. Something overcomes me, maybe it's the corn in the air, and I quickly lean in and kiss Josh on the cheek. I have never kissed him before. Some people are into that, being all enlightened and European or whatever, but I always thought that kisses were more sacred than that. Maybe that's why I didn't waste too much time with my crappy blips of exes.

"What was that for?" Josh asks, touching his cheek with his free hand.

"Needed to be done." I shrug.

"Mitchell *is* kind of romantic. What with a museum full of dolls ready to attack me and a palace made of corn."

Ha-ha. Always a kidder. I let go of Josh's hand and keep moving toward the Corn Palace. Of course he doesn't notice my missing hand. The one that used to be holding his. Not that my hand suddenly went missing.

Up close, the Palace is rather unbelievable, the entire facade elaborately decorated with dried cobs of corn in an array of autumn browns, yellows, and purples. The corn spells out MITCHELL CORN PALACE and the year, and the walls are covered in mosaics of tractors and animals made entirely of corn. "This is what the Mars' Cheese Castle should aspire to be," I say in wonder.

"Yeah, but think of the stench." Josh stands next to me and reaches his hand toward the corn. I smack it away out of respect.

"I guess cheese wouldn't work as well as corn. But, they could try a little harder to be spectacular." I'm disappointed in my cheese castle.

"Eh." Josh shrugs as though he's fine with the way things are. "Eh" is what Josh is all about right now. About his future, about us . . . I stomp my way through the doors.

Inside the Corn Palace are photos dating back to the early twentieth century from each year the Corn Palace was decorated. New designs are created yearly, painstakingly glued by hand to the building, truly putting the Mars' Cheese Castle to shame. I decide to buy some caramel corn from a stand inside the Palace, and as expected, it's the tastiest caramel corn I've ever had.

"The Mitchell Corn Palace delivers," I say through a mouthful of crispy, sweet, melty goodness. We buy a couple Corn Palace T-shirts from a small gift stand, take one last look at the history of corn display, and step outside to find a less corny dinner.

Across the street from the Corn Palace is a burger restaurant with an order window and benches outside for people-watching. We order a couple of cheeseburgers and fries, and park ourselves on a bench right on the main street. The town's not too busy, but there are enough people trying to take pictures that incorporate their family members and the entire Corn Palace that we are entertained for the duration of our meal.

When I can't stand the heat any longer, I declare, "It's time for the Enchanted World Doll Museum!"

"Nooooo!" Josh fake cries.

"Don't worry. I'll protect you." I stand up from the bench, and this time he takes my hand. We're so hot and sticky, I wonder if we'll ever be able to separate our hands again.

The doll museum is freakishly quiet inside, which would be awkward if we weren't the only people there. The lady at the entry desk (which is also the cash register for the gift shop) gives us a look that says don't touch anything, and directs us toward the turnstile that leads into the museum. Once we're through the museum door, Josh stands close behind me and wraps his arms around my stomach, digging his chin into my neck. I don't say anything, but it feels so good to be enveloped by him like this. I can smell his sweat, or maybe it's mine, but it's not ripe or unappealing. Maybe it's those pheromones we learned about in health class. Women are attracted to the manliness of sweat and all that.

We walk slowly, combined, and marvel at the doll scenes. Unlike other doll museums I've visited where you just see a doll in its pristine form, displayed as *a doll*, these dolls are intermingled with dolls of different ages and sizes and conditions, creating stories and scenes and, dare I say, interacting. In one case, a group of dolls anticipate the breaking of a piñata. Another lovingly offers us a glimpse at a doll wedding. In one, titled "Sunday Morning Service," corroding dolls dressed up in religious gear patiently await a sermon from a tiny pastor.

"This is the greatest place on earth," I muse. Huge dolls gallivant with miniscule ones, something my dolls would never do. Dolls with big glass eyes hang out with dolls whose eyes were merely applied with paint. Some dolls wear shoes, others go barefoot. It's a revolutionary dolly revelation! I'm sad when we get to the end of the displays and are released, once again, into the gift shop. I purchase a stack of postcards containing images of numerous doll dioramas, my favorite called "Saturday Night at the Rooming House," where various dolls of mismatched sizes wait patiently outside of a bathroom door while a fat, naked porcelain doll preens himself inside. Genius.

Outside of the doll museum, the setting sun glints off the Corn Palace flagpoles. "What do you want to do now?" I ask Josh dreamily in this almost surreal setting. It's only around eight o'clock, so if we checked into a hotel now, we'd have to think of ways to pass the time. But the town of Mitchell is closing up shop. I'm starting to envision me and Josh in a hotel room, when Josh says, "Let's keep driving? If I go to sleep anytime soon, I'm going to have doll nightmares." Were the dolls worth spoiling my hotel fantasy? I weigh the question as we load ourselves into the stuffy car. The warm air, the setting sun, and Elvis quickly lull my brain into submission.

So we drive toward the sunset, windows down; Elvis reruns fill the air. We drive as the stars bloom on the vast fabric of navy sky, passing miles of nothing, as bugs can't help but throw themselves at our windshield. We drive until my eyes close, until the tape flips again, until we finally come to a stop, in a town Josh tells me in a dreamy whisper is called Wall, and I float behind him as he holds my hand and leads me to a bed that's not mine and I fall asleep.

Went to Gavin's house for dinner. Well, sort of. He invited me over, rare, and I couldn't say no. Even after what happened the last time, over a year ago. Even after his dad threw that glass of beer, barely missed Gavin, splashed me but didn't cut me. He said his dad wouldn't be home. Everything's easier when the parents aren't home. But when we pulled up in my car, his dad's truck was there. Gavin told me to peel out. I didn't put the car into reverse fast enough for him, so he grabbed the shift and pulled it up too far and the car made a weird noise and sputtered, and I was afraid that we were stuck and that my car was broken. But then Gavin got it back in the right position and I backed out as quickly as I could manage, and we drove away really fast. He asked if McDonald's was OK. I wanted to open my mouth, but all I could do was nod.

CHAPTER FOURTEEN

The sun leaks through a slit in the room-darkening curtains, throwing a white slash on the wall. I sit up, and my eyes adjust to the hotel room, but not before my nose does. The room reeks of skunk, and I can't help but hold my hand over my face. Once I can see, I spy Josh in the second of two beds, asleep. I whip back the sheets, all my clothes still in their appropriate place on my body, and feel a nip of disappointment. I fumble my way into the bathroom and pray that the shower will wash the smell out of my nose. I expect to find bugs—or worse—when I pull back the shower curtain, but thankfully all I find is a tiny wrapped bar of soap and a mini bottle of shampoo/conditioner combo. The water heats up quickly, and I manage to lose the smell from my nose and the lameness of last night from my brain. I exit the bathroom with a towel around my middle, hoping that Josh will like what he sees. But Josh is still asleep, and I dress quickly to ensure the stank clings to as little of my body as possible. As a tribute to the fabulous town of Mitchell, I wear my new Corn Palace T-shirt, powder blue, kid-size for clinginess, which claims, THE WORLD'S ONLY CORN PALACE. IT'S A-MAIZE-ING! Not able to stand the stench any longer, I head to the door, which I'm slightly surprised to see Josh has bolted and chained; he seems too carefree to worry about safety. Maybe Wall didn't feel too savory after midnight.

The unlocking causes Josh to stir, so I call, "Good morning." A mumble comes from Josh's general direction. "I'm going outside," I tell him. "Need fresh air."

"Shower," is all he can say.

"Meet me outside when you're ready," I tell him, and then I enter the morning air of Wall, which, strangely, doesn't smell at all of the skunk stench in our room. Glad I didn't think to look under the beds.

We're on the second floor of a motel, and the balcony view is a dusty parking lot and a road strewn with fast-food restaurants. A few rooms down, a family props their door open with a cooler. Two bright blond boys calculatedly drop ice cubes over the railing. I look over the balcony to see a puddle surrounded by pigeons. "I almost got him! Didja see that?" the taller boy shrieks at the smaller one. I pray they don't look over at me to join in on their merry animal abuse game, but luckily Josh emerges from behind the clunky motel door and gives me a warm, kinda sexy smile. "Morning, Sunshine." I smile back and hope those

115

little Aryans think we're together. As if they care. I could step on them anyway.

After we check out from the tiny front office (and decide not to partake in what smells like last week's free coffee), we head to the car. Our destination is only a few blocks away, but we drive based on the barrenness of the town. Wall Drug, it turns out, is not exactly a drugstore but a full-on city block of *stuff*. Unlike the House on the Rock, however, this is mostly stuff you can buy. And most of it is stamped with WALL DRUG in some form.

Hungry and groggy, we make our way to the sprawling restaurant, a counter-service-seat-yourself kind of place, with a sign claiming to seat 530. Quite a few tables are *ocupado*, but not enough to feel crowded by the other guests. Josh and I order coffee and some cinnamon-sugar doughnuts, and Josh adds, "Why don't you add in some of that free ice water?" He charms the girl behind the counter, name-tagged Nadia.

Josh doesn't like to talk much before his morning coffee, so I look around at all of the crap they have hanging from the walls and ceiling. I read the brochure in the plastic holder on the table, explaining how Wall Drug began as a simple rest stop for those needing a drink and turned into a mecca of kitsch (my words, not theirs). After breakfast, I expect to be wowed by the hilarity that is Wall Drug, but as Josh and I stroll through store after store of stuff we don't need and don't really want, I feel let down. There's a scuzziness to the place that's not exactly funny.

Josh and I choose a few items to show the world we have indeed been to Wall Drug—bumper stickers, T-shirts, a mug. As we pay, I detect an Eastern European accent on our cashier, a ripe-looking girl named Polina. Underneath her name, her name tag reads, "Kiev."

"My great-grandparents were from Kiev," I tell her. She gives me a slight smile and nod, and continues ringing up our spoils. I fill the silence. "I noticed a lot of name tags list different countries."

"Yes, we all came over together," she says, friendly, but not overly warm. She explains how Wall Drug recruits people from other countries to work here for months at a time. They all live together in a little apartment complex. "We do it so we can see America," she says.

"So where else have you been?" I ask.

"Nowhere. This is all we have seen for three months." She tips her head to showcase what she has seen of our fabulous country. She doesn't try to hide her lack of enthusiasm.

"Will you get to go anywhere other than Wall? Before you go home?" It seems so tragic that someone would come all this way to experience life in another country, and all they get to see is the inside of this stankhole filled with obnoxious tourists picking up stuffed jackalopes and commemorative spoons while they're on their way to somewhere else.

"A few of us are going to Las Vegas when we're done in a month." She sounds excited.

Vegas. The real America? As real as Wall Drug. At least she won't be working.

That's when Josh interjects his charm into the conversation and tells Polina about the crazy times he and his dad have had in Vegas. I glaze over, having heard his dad regale us with the same stories in an almost desperately cool manner over the flaming table at Benihana's Japanese Steak House. Plus, how many times do I have to witness Josh flirting with someone? Me included?

I finally catch Josh's eye when I see him write something on a Wall Drug brochure and slip it across the counter to Polina. He nods in acknowledgment—it's time to go—and I walk away to wait by the door without a good-bye to my new foreign acquaintance. I step out onto Wall's main street, which isn't nearly as quaint or, um, corny as Mitchell, and instead has a more dusty, used feel. I'm ready to get the heck out of Wall. The idea that there are people flown in from other countries, essentially kept prisoner in Dead Street America and forced to shill crap is überdisturbing. I jump a bit when Josh plants his hand on my shoulder. "Ready to book?" he asks.

"Beyond ready." As we walk to the car, I poke. "So you gave that girl your phone number? Even though we don't live near here and she's from a land far, far away?" I should hide my snark, but I don't get why being together on the road, in hotels, is not swaying Josh in any way toward me romantically. Maybe I should have a bumper sticker made: WHY THE HECK DON'T YOU WANT ME? Not as catchy as the Wall Drug ones, but maybe it would be effective if I stuck it to my butt. Or to Josh's forehead.

"I didn't give her my phone number," Josh defends. "I wrote down some of the must-sees of Vegas. That would have been tacky, dontcha think?"

"Tacky how?"

"Since I'm here with you and all." He says this as he gets into the car and starts it, so there's no opportunity for me to see his expression. With me *how*? I want to ask, but it's time to navigate the frig out of Wall, and it's still too early in the day for me to try and have *that* conversation. I've held off for four years, haven't I?

"Hasta la pasta, Wall!" Josh calls out the window as he peels out of the parking lot. It's dorky lines like this that make me like Josh so much. And coming from those lips, delicious looking, always just a little chapped because he's too guy to wear Chapstick, well, the dorkiness just gets filtered out.

We head south of Wall toward Badlands National Park. "I love how that sounds. Badlands!" Josh yells and flashes the devil sign like we're at a cheese-rock arena concert.

119

As we drive into the park, we notice a cavalcade of Corvettes driving in the opposite direction. New ones, classic ones, all driven by older men and women. "Must be some kind of club. Like, retirees who like to drive Corvettes," I guess. A particularly sleek iridescent purple 'Vette rumbles by.

"Maybe they're vets who drive 'Vettes? You know, like war veterans?" Josh guesses, with a smile in his eyes at his cleverness.

"Or maybe they're not war vets. Maybe they're veterinarians," I pontificate.

He ignores me. "That's the life, man. Not having to work, slick car, driving anywhere you want to go." Josh pulls the Eurosport into a parking spot at a scenic overlook, where more Corvettes are pulling away.

"Isn't that what you're doing now? Aside from the slickness of the car. And you didn't even have to fight in a war—or work with animals—or work at all, for that matter to earn the right to retire," I point out. Sometimes Josh's rich-daddy side rears its ugly head, and I have to take him down a notch.

"I'm working." He's defensive. "Once I get the band together, write songs, tour. That's work."

"Mmmhmmm." We step out to read some of the park signage that explains the lore of the Badlands, which were so named by the Lakota Indians and early French trappers because of the varied harshness of the landscape, from vast empty prairies to rainbow-colored rock formations that made the land difficult to cross. I look across the endless low hills and imagine a time when roads didn't cut through nature. The only way from point A to point B was up and down, up and down, slipping on rocks, tasting the dry air. I smack my tongue and am thankful for the cooler of pop in the car.

Josh and I decide to make a plan for the next couple of days, so we don't miss out on anything we want to see but so we also don't forget that we have a final destination. That forces me to look at my phone. No reception. Well, then I must not be missing any calls, so there's no need to feel guilty, I assure myself.

We choose to spend the day driving and hiking around the Badlands, then spend tonight in Deadwood, again be-cause of the name. (Josh claims that it sounds like a "sexy Wild West town. You know, prostitutes were legal there up until the 1980s?" How he knew this charming fact, I have no idea. Nor do I want to.) After that, well, that's as far as we got with our plan.

I can't say I've ever been a nature girl, but this Badlands place is pretty sweet. It's not all big trees covering my head, making me wonder what's dangling above me. The Bad-lands basically call out, "Don't bother. You'd never make it across alive," making it perfectly acceptable to drive around on man-made roads and watch the nature from the safety and (albeit un-air-conditioned) comfort of our car. Periodically, we can park and walk on a gravelly path, well-marked by signage of just how far we can go to maintain contact with civilization.

It's on one of these walks where, uninterrupted by the din of the open car windows or the curse of the cell phone reception, I get up the nerve to have the talk.

Josh sits down on a large tan rock, smoothed by thousands of butts before him. I scooch him over with my hip, and we sit, back to back supporting each other.

"Beautiful day, eh?" he asks. I look around at the striped hills, the way the colors change from the sandy brown bottom to a pinkish red layer, then top off with a gray cap. No cities to be seen. No suburban sprawl. No prepackaging.

"I guess," I answer. It is beautiful—I know it is—but it's hard for me to experience it as beauty instead of just anxiety at the thought of having to conquer it. Or maybe it's not conquering "it" that worries me, but "him."

Then I notice something. It's an unnatural color, a red that's a little too bright, too harsh, to be part of this world, just a little farther down the path. I un-lean myself from Josh and head toward the color, which stains the side of a rock about half my height and three times as wide. Graffiti. At first, I'm appalled that someone would deface nature, but rocks aren't really nature, are they? I mean, they're not alive, not unless they're a donkey that magically got turned into a rock.

And who bothers to bring spray paint with them when they're driving through a national park?

But when I read and discover what it says, I forget my disgust, my curiosity. Because this message was meant for me. A simple heart, with a cupid's arrow piercing from bottom left to top right, surrounds the dripping, but legible letters, telling me, DON'T STOP NOW. A message. A mantra. For the road. For Josh. For the quest. I believe it.

The crunch of the earth behind me signals Josh's approach. I turn to see him, hair tucked behind his ear, orange T-shirt off, hanging from the back of his loose shorts. Framed by the untouchable Badlands, *he* is nature. He is all that I want to see and experience right now.

I walk up to him and run my fingers over the brown stubble on his cheeks. My red hair looks foreign in the reflection of his sunglasses. "Hey," I breathe.

"Hey." I see his eyebrow cock in question. I lean forward and gently brush his lips with mine. "What . . . ?" he begins to say, and I kiss him again, more pressure, more urgent. He kisses back. I'm surprised and elated and melting into him. His hand is on my shoulder, my back, and mine is on his, his bare skin, taut and sticky from the heat. We kiss, a kiss I've dreamed about for years, even while kissing other guys. While he was with other girls. A kiss worth waiting for. Then Josh pulls away.

"Wait . . . ," he says again.

" 'Don't stop now,' " I quote the rock.

"I don't know, Lil. I don't think . . ."

"You don't think what?" I ask, getting defensive, my big ol' quest in danger of being crushed. By a rock, perhaps.

"I just don't think we should." He looks down and kicks his foot against my rock.

"Why not?" I sound like a kid.

"I just like you too much, I guess." His answer is barely an answer.

"That's stupid," I say. *You're stupid*, I think. I'm stupid, I know. "I get it. Forget it."

"Lil, you know I love you. I have too much respect for you to change us."

"Too much respect? Do people actually say that? Do you actually believe that?" I lean against my rock, letting it support me.

"If it's true, they do." He shrugs.

"Have you ever wanted to?" I don't feel the need to elaborate. If he doesn't know what I'm talking about, then he hasn't wanted to.

"Well, yeah, I mean, I'm a guy."

"That you are." I say it like an insult.

"Lil, don't be like that." He moves to put his hand on my shoulder, and I dodge it. "Let's keep on going. Our mission. For Penny."

"It's a *quest*," I scold him. "*My* quest. I'm just using you for your car." I try to hurt him. He's not buying or else he doesn't care, and he gives a sly smile. I want to press it. *If you love me, then how can you not want to love me more? If we kissed, why can't we just keep kissing? Not stopping ever?* But it hurts to be stopped mid-kiss, love or no love.

"Well, then, you want a ride?" I swear I see a light glint off his teeth, and I can't stay mad. Embarrassed, maybe. Disappointed. Definitely. But I'm not entirely convinced this moment is over.

I take a phone picture of the marked rock before we leave, to remember the personal message it left me.

"Don't stop now."

I vow not to.

• • •

We're going away for spring break. I can't believe it. We're going to Disney World. It looks happy in pictures. I need a new bathing suit, my mom said. She wanted to order one on QVC, but I said what if it doesn't fit and they don't let us return it. She said I was right, and she took me to Kohl's because she got a 30-percent-off coupon in the mail. Me and Annabelle got two new bathing suits each. One of mine is even a bikini. I don't even look that bad in mine. Annabelle even said so. One week away in warmth and sun and bikinis. One week away where I have to tell Gavin how much I'm going to miss him. Even if I'm not so sure it's true.

CHAPTER FIFTEEN

The Badlands Rock Experience replays over and over in my head as Elvis can't help falling in love (again) on the stereo. Why can't Josh help falling in love with *me*? Being together is so easy. We love to talk, but we don't have to talk, and we're perfectly aligned in height. Isn't that how things are supposed to be? But if it was really love, wouldn't we be planning some sort of future together instead of the vagueness of me going to school one state over and him going wherever his rock star fantasy believes him to be going? I don't like to think about it. Us apart.

I scooch my way across the bench seat to the slim middle seat only fitting for half a human and click on the lap belt. Josh takes his right arm from the steering wheel and drapes it over my shoulder. I lean into him, resting my head on his nicely padded shoulder. We've sat like this a million times. Is it different now that we've kissed? In my mind maybe, but in his . . . I don't get it.

Trying to appeal to his guyly ego, I say, "Tell me about

the band," and Josh lights up. His favorite subject: The Band. Josh has been in various incarnations of said band since I've known him, but rarely are they anything more than a few random guys getting together in Josh's basement to jam, playing other bands' songs and breaking up over "creative differences." A precious few have stayed together long enough to actually play a show, usually just a local gig at youth centers or (insert town name here) Day's festivals. Always covers.

Josh talks about the new band he plans to form. He'll advertise on Craigslist: Bassist Needed. Post flyers downtown. Auditions, of course there will be auditions. I can come if I want, if I'm in town. He's always respected my opinion musically, which, admittedly, is somewhat of a burden. Because, and I would never tell Josh this, I don't actually love his music. At first, when I was just a freshman, it was so cool to sit in his basement while he and a bunch of guys would jam or practice. Sometimes there'd be a whole group of us, girlfriends of the musicians, plus me, girl friend. The other girls would attempt to get up and dance, to show their guys how into the music they were, which would ultimately just piss off Josh. "It's not that kind of music!" he'd yell, and the girls would sulk back to the couches and talk crap about Josh for the rest of the session. No one took the music as seriously as Josh did, which is why he never found the right mix of musicians to form a true band. Plus, his sound isn't exactly radio friendly. Maybe college radio friendly, but nothing close to mainstream. One of Josh's favorite activities was to have me come over and watch him experiment with his, as he put it, "musical flavors." And for a while, yeah, it was interesting. The way he could just push a button on his computer and it would add a melodic beep or speed up the song or take a sneeze and turn it into a rhythm section. He could pick up any instrument and play it decently; some he mastered. As we became closer and I didn't feel as desperate for him to like me (partly because I could tell he already really liked me, but also because I could tell that he really didn't like me *like that. Yet*), I started bringing my homework or a *Buffy* comic, just to give me something to do so I didn't go completely insane listening to his abstract creations (which he barely noticed because he was so into his music making). We work well together even when we're not working together.

Now as we drive, my head on his shoulder, he blathers on about The Band tentatively titled Carpet Tongue, or Pretello, or Fromage (French for "cheese"). The names change daily, sometimes hourly. Josh isn't one to commit. To bands or to girls, I guess. Maybe that's what makes him so attractive? But not attracted?

I'm surprised (but not all that much) to find that I've fallen asleep when Josh wakes me with a tickle to my scalp. "We're here," he whispers. Here is Deadwood, a town immortalized by a TV show and remembered as a debaucherous Wild West town, the place where Wild Bill Hickok was shot in the back while playing cards. I know this because I have always had a fascination with historical celebrity deaths. For instance, it was said that the original Siamese twins, Chang and Eng (who helped change the common lingo from "conjoined" to "Siamese" by their heritage), died with Chang the first to go and Eng sitting there, dead twin attached, knowing, waiting, for his time to come, while at the same time mourning his brother's death and possibly savoring the only moment of his life when he was truly alone. Hickok's death was a good story because he was a suspicious man who always refused to sit with his back to a door. A compulsive gambler, he couldn't resist a poker game, even if it meant taking the last remaining spot at the table one fateful day (and, thus, facing the room and not the door). He even tried to switch seats with the other players at the table, but no luck. In the end—his end—he was shot in the back by a guy named Jack McCall, probably over some petty Wild West issue, like a five-dollar debt. The cards Hickok held in his hand are today still known as the Dead Man's Hand. Or so the story goes.

I've got tons of stories like that stuffed into my memory. And don't get me started on killers like Lizzie Borden. Or Typhoid Mary. I can't remember the Pythagorean theorem to save my life, but give me a good serial killer or gruesome death, and I'd ace that exam. Those are the kind of stories I'd like to write or movies I'd like to make someday. I'm hoping college professors will be more open to gore than high school English teachers. Not that I've ever shared the really gory stuff with them or with Josh. I haven't exactly shared any of my stories with Josh, since the one time I tried he was so distracted by his new wah-wah pedal he could barely get through the first page without fiddling with his guitar. And if he did actually manage to finish, what if he felt the same way about my stories as I do about his experimental music? Better I keep them to myself until I know he's listening. If we could get just *thatmuchcloser*, I bet I could get him to listen.

Deadwood's main street holds a layer of tack underneath its Western exterior. Casinos make up the majority of the storefronts, so we stop into one with signs blaring, OWNED BY ACADEMY AWARD–WINNING ACTOR KEVIN COSTNER. Kev's movie posters hang everywhere, and signed photos line the bar. The security guard stationed by the door, to ensure we don't slip even one quarter prematurely into a slot machine, tells us that there is no gambling for anyone under twenty-one. Josh, quarter in hand, says, "I don't know how Kevin Costner would feel about this." The guard gives us the "out" thumb, and we leave, but not before Josh calls back, "Kevin Costner's a douche!"

Mt. Moriah Cemetery bus tours are offered at little wooden stands on every downtown street corner, so Josh buys us a couple tickets and we climb aboard a minibus that takes us on the short trip to the local famous cemetery.

The bus is full, which surprises me a little since it feels like we're in the middle of nowhere. Apparently, large families and senior citizens like to be nowhere, too.

Above the bus driver's seat is a photo of the driver with—surprise!—Kevin Costner. Other Deadwood-related photos and browned newspaper clippings line the bus ceiling. The driver, who calls himself Gentle Jim, regales us with Deadwood tales of yore over his crackly headset mic while the bus creeps up steep, winding streets toward the cemetery that looms above the town. My favorite story is about a man named Potato Creek Johnny, who found the largest gold nugget in them thar Black Hills. Just because I like the name Potato Creek Johnny. The most horrific story is of the hill just below the actual cemetery. Unmarked, it's filled with the bodies of what were once Deadwood's large Chinese population. Wild West, indeed.

We gladly exit the bus beside the cemetery for a quick look around. The bus hoard gravitates toward Wild Bill's grave, marked with a bust of his head, but I walk to the edge to peer over at the small town of Deadwood below.

"Can you imagine"—Josh saunters up next to me to marvel at the town that once was—"the streets of Deadwood? No law. A six-shooter on your belt and a prostitute on your arm?" Josh looks whimsical, as if he's reliving his past life's glory days.

"And syphilis in your pants," I add.

"That, too!" He continues to look jokily dreamy.

Josh takes my hand, and we stroll among the old grave-stones, some of young children. Cemeteries, especially old ones, are filled with stories. Just a name, a beginning and an expiration date, maybe some spare, kind words, could inspire an entire novel. "Roy Grimshaw. Born August 6, 1879. Died November 13, 1889." So long ago. Just ten years old. What was his story? "Seth Bullock. Pioneer. Martha His Wife." Was "pioneer" Seth's job? Seth doesn't seem like a very old-timey name. And all Martha was qualified for was "wife"? I take a few pictures of headstones, saving them for the day I might need inspiration for a book.

Gentle Jim herds the crowd back into the bus, and we make our way down in an equally bumpy, albeit not as lively (cemeteries will do that to you), manner. Once re-turned to even ground, Josh and I decide to chow at an all-you-can-eat buffet at a family-friendly casino. Josh piles seafood onto his plate, as it is Surf and Turf Night, while I opt for some soup and salad, and then design my own one-of-everything dessert platter. It is during our third round of dessert debauchery that my cell phone rings. I jump a bit, having forgotten the possibility of reception in an actual town. A new, unfamiliar area code and number appear.

"Maybe I shouldn't get it," I say tentatively, feeling less vulnerable as the distance between me and home expands.

"Maybe you shouldn't," Josh agrees through a spray of cake crumbs.

"But maybe I should," I waffle.

"Maybe you should," he says, spitting more crumbs.

"Thanks for your sage advice." I pause, then involuntarily answer. "Hello?"

"Lil?" A quiet, nervous voice asks, and I know in an instant who it is.

"Penny!" I'm more relieved than I expected, unearthing the slight fear I had of the possibility that she had, just maybe, really been kidnapped.

"Yeah, it's me. How are you?" Penny asks, as though she just called to chat. Queen of denial.

"Never mind how I am, dear, how are you?" My tone is adult and scoldy.

"Pretty good," is all she answers. Her breathy obliviousness is grating.

"Yeeeaaahh. So, have you talked to anyone lately?" I want to know if the FBI chase is over, if her parents and the cops and the FBI already know where she is. I want to know if I'm in the clear. I want to know if she gets that this is a big deal.

"Nope. Have you?" She's so lackadaisical, I could kick her ass through the phone. I stab a tiny pink cake with my fork.

"As a matter of fact, I've talked to a bunch of people. Your dad, your mom, the police. Oh, and the FBI called me the other day." I ooze sarcasm.

"What about Gavin?" she asks, completely missing the shock value of the list.

"Are you kidding me? Who gives a floating turd about Gavin? The *FBI* called me."

"Did you tell them anything?" she asks, sounding less nervous than she should. Almost intrigued, even.

"No. Did you want me to tell them something?" I'm so confused.

"No." Penny sounds confused, too. Hesitant. Like maybe she does want them to know. Like maybe she told me in the first place because she thought I *would* tell. She really hasn't had any good friendships, has she?

"You know, you could tell them," I push. Then I hear a guy's voice in the background of Penny's phone. "Who's that?" I ask.

"That's Ethan."

"Ethan from Disney World? From Portland?"

"Yeah," is all she says. So glad we can have this long chat, what with no phone charger and all.

"Are you at his house now?" I prod.

"Yeah. He's been great." She has a smile in her voice. "I kind of have to go now."

Why the hell did she call me? "Is there something you wanted, Penny? You know, seeing as you called and all?" I'm so annoyed that I'm at her whim. Without any acknowledgment of what I've done or been through for her. Without even a thank-you.

"Lil?" she starts. Pause.

"Yeah?" I'm waiting.

"Don't tell anyone still, OK?"

"I haven't yet, have I?" Doesn't she get that I already could have? Does she not know who the FBI is?

"You're a really good friend," Penny says.

Zing. Ouch. Fine.

I'm completely thrown off by the statement. So thrown that I forget to ask where exactly Ethan's house is or what his last name is or anything important. By the time I remember all of the things I need to know to complete my quest, Penny mumbles through the end of a bad connection, and the phone goes silent.

"So I notice you're not writing down an address or anything. She's calling you back, right? Or now you've got a number you can call her at?" Josh inquires. He grabs the fork out of my hand, at the end of which are the remains of a once-lovely cake, and stuffs the mush into my mouth.

"She told me I was a really good friend," I say, staring ahead at the buffet, the cornucopia of foods blurring into a flavored rainbow.

"Bitch," Josh chides. "How dare she?"

"She didn't even care that the FBI is after me! She just wanted to know if Gavin knew anything."

"One-track mind, that kid." He talks through the cake bits in his mouth.

"I should call her back now. Get the address." I find the first number in my recent calls folder and press the call button. The phone doesn't even ring but goes directly to voicemail. A relaxed, deep voice says, "Hi, this is Ethan. Leave me a message." Beep.

"Hey, Ethan, um, this is Lillian Erlich. I'm a friend of Penny's. She really needs to call me when you get this message. Please? My number is . . ."

I close my phone, breathe in deeply through my nose, and then go off. "I can't wait to get to Portland so I can flick her stupid face and make *her* talk to the FBI and the cops and her parents!" I'm seething at the audacity of her calling me a good friend. Why couldn't she just let me be mad at her, at her irresponsibility, her victimhood, her sucking of me into her pathetic world? I take my palm and smash down several tiny desserts on my plate, one at a time like Whac-A-Mole.

"That looks fun," Josh enthuses, and we spend the next five minutes trying to avoid each other's hands as we attempt to smash the rest of the treats. "We're getting The Look." Josh nods to a buffet worker giving us the stink eye. "Let's go." Josh drops a couple bucks on the table as a cleanup tip, and we step into the warm night air. "What now?" he asks.

I'm buzzing from the twenty desserts and the conversation with Penny. My quest has turned into a vendetta. All I want to do is get to Portland, find Penny, and tell her what an idiot she is. Then I'll force her to see that faking her own kidnapping to avoid a complete bastard of a boyfriend—or is it to get his attention? Or her parents' attention? She's sure got my attention. Whatever her motivation, it is NOT NORMAL.

"Do you feel like driving?" I ask Josh. "Maybe all night?"

"We'll see how far we can go on sugar and caffeine. We can always sleep in the car. It's a pretty big backseat." Josh waggles his eyebrows.

You should know, I think, but brush it away. No time for those kind of thoughts right now. *Don't stop now*, I think, and I'm ready to hit the road.

· · ·

I met someone. In Disney World. My age. Really nice. Too nice? Ethan. His name's Ethan. He makes me laugh. He asks me why I cover my mouth when I smile, and I tell him because I have one tooth that's crooked. He asks to see and holds my chin. I shouldn't let him, but I do. And I smile without covering it up.

CHAPTER SIXTEEN

We peel out of Deadwood with a "Yee ha!" and cross the Wyoming border in a half hour. Still not having crashed from the sugar rush, we shout our state-crossing chant. The view from the Eurosport—the part of it that's not obscured by the ever-growing collection of bug splat on our windshield—is of never-ending land and sky. Mountains are everywhere, something you just don't see in the flatlands of Illinois (hence the Wisconsin insult "Flatlanders" to our "Cheeseheads"). The waning moon exposes peaks and crags enough so we know we're not anywhere near home. I imagine a road on another planet. Maybe Venus. Or Mars. Don't know. Never paid too much attention in science class when we studied planets in elementary school. I wanted to be interested, because they were so pretty, but they just seemed so far away.

Speaking of far away, I'm feeling a distance between me and Josh that's somewhere between the size of Mount Rushmore (which we'll try to see on our return trip) and the Grand Canyon (which we'll miss on this trip completely without a mega detour). Josh and I stopped at a gas station just over the state line to fill up, and he picked up several cans of a repulsive energy drink to keep him awake. The chemicals have him spouting off some ridiculous idea for a concept album, but I can barely hear him over the *whoosh* of the wind. I was hoping this night could turn into our time to talk (again), since we've managed to do so little of that even with all of this concentrated time together. But the heat of the day hasn't cooled down enough, not yet, and the car amplified any and all sun that it connected with. The tornado of air and the drone of Josh lulls me into sleep quickly. It never takes much.

I am awakened at one point by Josh hollering out the state chant for Montana but fall hard and fast into a deep sleep. Sometime later, I'm awakened by the state cry for Wyoming again, much less boisterous than the last cry, but I'm still zonked. I finally wake on my own to the orange glow of the sunrise splashing through the window. My neck is kinked to the left where it hung all night against the headrest, and there is drool on the seat belt. The air outside is thick with mist, so thick that all I can tell about our surroundings is that (a) they're not moving, so neither are we, and (b) we're in a parking lot because I can faintly see other cars nearby and yellow lines on the ground.

I locate Josh immediately by the snore/snort from the backseat and turn to find him curled up into a childlike ball. I open the door, which I'm happy to see Josh locked in an effort to keep out any hobos or hook-handed maniacs. The air outside is finally cool, and the mist is so thick, it's wet. I catch a hazy view of a wooden sign, alerting me to our whereabouts: Old Faithful Visitors' Center in Yellowstone National Park. I remember hearing about Old Faithful as a kid, but it always sounded to me like something out of another era, like Smokey the Bear or the Hoover Dam.

The visitors' center has a bathroom, thank god, which I use and attempt to wash off the seat lines that appear to be permanently etched into my face. My red hair still surprises me, although I don't think it would fool anyone in a lineup. Has the FBI figured it out? Do they know I'm hiding the truth? Do I really need to worry in an area remote enough that I don't even get cell phone reception? I'm starting to think that the nature in the national parks is a good thing.

I pull my phone out of my pocket to double-check the reception (or lack thereof) and see the battery is running low. Not warning message low, but less than half. I turn the phone completely off, since all it's good for right now is its clock and camera.

Once I'm as preened as one can be in a national park bathroom, I stroll around the visitors' center and read the story of Old Faithful, named so because its spout of boiling water shoots up so predictably. There are numerous quaint anecdotes about how back in the 1800s, people used the geyser to do laundry, but only for cotton items. It ripped wool to shreds. Odd. I'd think wool would be hardier.

My mind wanders to the name Old Faithful, and I try to pound some sort of symbol for my quest out of it. Is Penny Old Faithful because at least she's predictably pathetic and needy and does absurd things, albeit never as previously absurd as faking her own kidnapping? Is Josh Old Faithful because I can always count on him for a laugh, a hug, and a fantastical conversation about a band that will never be? Or am I Old Faithful because I stand by these two, in sickness and in (mental) health, richer or poorer (Josh's richer to my poorer), grope fest or no? Nothing sexy about being Old Faithful.

I move out of the visitors' center, annoyed at myself for starting a metaphor that I can't finish. The mist has cleared considerably as the wind picks up, and I see Josh, Old Faithfully Shirtless, stretching his arms outside of the car. "Morning, Sunshine," he calls, and the few other early morning nature enthusiasts in the lot look to find the sunshine in question. I tip my fake cap to Josh and walk over.

"What time did we get here?" I ask. Josh starts to dig through the car for a shirt and finds one that reads, FEAR THE BADGER. "Can you get one for me?" I request. He sifts through the shirts, picks one up, reads it, throws it back down, picks up another, repeat, until he finds one suitable enough for me. It's red and reads, WISCONSIN IS FOR CHEESE LOVERS.

"Around five," he tells me, as I discreetly lean into the car and pull off my old shirt to slip into the new one. I hope Josh watches. He doesn't. "What time is it now?"

"I don't know. I turned off my phone to save batteries. Must be after eight, though, because that's what time the visitors' center opens."

"Gotta drain the snake," Josh declares, and with his toothbrush and toothpaste in hand, he heads for the visitors' center bathroom. I check my own breath (not pleasant) and opt for a piece of sugarless mint gum. I hate brushing my teeth in a public sink. Spitting. Blow-drying my face when there are no paper towels.

Josh makes it back to the car in less time than it would take me to squat and flush, and inhales his newly minty freshness through the sides of his teeth. "Want to check out ye Ol' Faithful?" Josh asks. I laugh, and he presents his hand for me to hold. We walk together in this familiar, misleading manner to a sort of observation pier that looks over a barren area with a steamy hole in the ground. Surrounding the desolation is a never-ending forest of pine trees. Or maybe they're firs. Or maybe firs *are* pine trees. An old couple, wrinkly and hunched, stand nearby in matching yellow raincoats. The man leans on a cane, and the woman smiles at us. "Such a lovely young couple," she creaks.

"Thank you." Josh bows proudly. My old faithful friend. Friend friend friend. Blah. My grump is short lived when a loud eruption makes me jump. Out of the steamy hole

144

shoots the geyser, over a hundred feet into the air, like a supersize fireman's hose. It sprays for half a minute, and I become unimpressed. It's just hot water ejaculating from a hole in the ground. I don't get it. I think it reads my thoughts because the wind shifts and the tower of water starts to lean the opposite way toward the pier. The elder couple pull up their hoods, and a few seconds later we're showered with a spray of warm water. The geyser itself is still erect (Erect? Ejaculates? Where is my head?), but the wind has made it clear that nature is to be marveled at, and we are merely puny humans next to this unstoppable, *faithful* force.

Just because something's faithful doesn't mean it's predictable.

• • •

I was so happy. For a week and a day. But now my cheek hurts and my stomach hurts, and I need to get to the store to buy a new foundation to match my tan and cover up my cheek. If only I had just waited until Gavin came over to give him his souvenir coconut patties. If only I hadn't gone to his house and saw him and his dad fighting. If only I didn't see his dad punch him in the stomach. If only I hadn't been there as his getaway car. If only I'd been the one to get away.

CHAPTER SEVENTEEN

Back on the road, I sit in the middle seat as we cruise the required low speed limit through Yellowstone. The radio is off, and the slowness means wind can't overpower our speech.

Josh starts, "So I had this idea while I was driving last night. . . ." My interest peaked, I'm certain he's about to finally reveal his undying devotion to me. Or at least that he'd like to make out some time. But instead he says, "Tambourines, man. Gotta get some tambourines." Logically.

In the past, Old Faithful would let Josh drone on about the fascinating subject of the tambourine, its origin, famous tambourinists throughout history, the different sound qualities among particular brands, but maybe *I* feel like talking today. So I interrupt. "You know, I've been thinking a lot about school lately."

Josh is quiet for a minute. "Oh?" he finally asks, in a tone that's not angry, but definitely perturbed.

"Yeah. All of this driving and nature, it's making me

think a lot about writing versus film. You know, the written word versus visual expression. I don't know how I'll pick my major."

"Yeah," is all Josh can say, so I continue.

"Winthorp is supposed to have both great creative-writing and film teachers, so I'm hoping I'll just know once I meet them, you know? Kismet, and all that?"

"Sure." Josh looks out his window. I can't tell if he's even listening, so I try to make the conversation a little more interactive (more interactive than already ending each sentence with a question). "So, if you ever do go to college, do you think you'll major in music?"

"What?" Josh springs to indignant life. "Hell, no. I'm not going to college. Any creativity you have just gets sucked out by the bureaucratic machine," he tells me. "The only way to make *real* music is to live *real* life." He speaks as though it's the gospel, as if of course I'm thinking the same thing. Which I'm not.

"Right. Because actually learning how to play an instrument correctly would do so much damage to your music. God forbid you try at something instead of just talking about it." I know it's hitting below the belt, but he completely insulted me and my bureaucratic machine.

"I don't just talk about music. I create it," Josh says defensively.

"In your dad's basement. And rarely does it escape those wood-paneled walls." I continue my attack, setting aside the fact that I actually believe in Josh and his bizarre music. But how can he dismiss my future when all I've done is support his?

"I thought you liked my music." He practically pouts.

"Did you even hear what you said before? You totally crapped on my life."

"No, I didn't," he says, shocked.

"Um, creativity getting sucked out? Bureaucracy and all that? I'm going to college. And I believe that it's going to help me creatively, not stifle me just because I might be learning something along the way."

"Well, I didn't mean *you*." We're still crawling along at the speed limit, when someone in an SUV zooms around us on a single lane, no passing road. Josh jams his middle finger up high out the window. "What a dick!" He turns to me to watch me agree. And I do.

"Yeah, what a dick." I scowl and continue where I left off, "You know, Josh, it seems like there are a whole lot of things you think don't apply to me. Like, everyone who goes to college is a drone, except me. And every girl is worth flirting with, except me. And holding hands means something to everyone else in the world, except us. I thought I did, but I don't get you at all."

Josh sighs loudly, not angrily but thoughtfully, pauses, and pulls the car into a scenic view spot. Out the Eurosport window is an open prairie surrounded by the backdrop of evergreens (Pines? Oh, shut up!). Josh shuts off the

149

engine, unclicks his seat belt, and turns toward me. "Lil, don't you like holding hands with me?"

"You know I do, Josh. You've always known. And I think that kiss from the other day should more than tell you the answer." I look down at my hands and pick at a cuticle. Josh rests his hand on top of mine, and I stop.

"Well, I like holding hands with you, too. That's why I do it. Your hands aren't clammy or hot or icy-dead feeling. They're always so smooth and comfy." Great. I have smooth, comfy hands. Maybe I should go into hand modeling instead of writing. "And I liked kissing you, too, if you didn't notice. I mean, I kissed you back, didn't I?" *Oh.* "It's just"—and here comes the *but*—"like I said before: I don't want to ruin what we have."

"That's cliché and a cop-out, and you know it. Why would adding something good take away from what we have?" I look up at his melty brown eyes. They look back at me defeated.

"Have you ever known me to have a good relationship with a girl after we hook up?"

"Well, no, but if you did, then we wouldn't be hanging out now. It just takes one good one to stick."

"Maybe it's not them. Maybe it's me."

"You are so full of clichés today. How could it be you if you're always dumping them? Are you saying that maybe you have a compulsive dumping habit? Should we call Dumpers Anonymous?"

"Yeah, well, about that. I don't think Dumpers Anonymous would take me, since I've never actually technically dumped a girl," Josh mumbles.

"Wait—what? Really? How?" I'm shocked. Josh has had double, maybe triple digits' worth of girlfriends, or at least hookups, since I've known him, and he never once did the breaking up?

"Truth?" he asks, looking at me sincerely.

"Truth." I nod.

"I think I bored them to the point of dumpage. The initial me"—he waves his hands over himself, acknowledging his undeniable beauty—"gets the girl no problem. But after the hands-on exhibit and we start talking, they just don't want to hear about my music and stuff." While I guess I could kind of empathize with the girls, Josh's passion for his music more than makes up for the actual content. At least most of the time. And the combination of the physical with the musical devotion?

"They're idiots," I assure him. "Maybe they didn't want to hear you talk." I try to lighten it up. "Maybe they were using you for your body. It is in rather usable condition."

"True." He perks up a bit. "So is yours, you know," he adds with a cornered smile. I blush.

"You think so?" I ask, looking down at his hand still on mine.

"Most definitely," he says, in an intonation I have only heard reserved for waitresses and cashiers. I look up again, expecting something, but not at all what I see. Behind Josh through the window is an enormous beast. "Oh my god!" I jump and Josh turns around to see a two-thousand-pound male bison peering into our window. His head is half the size of the Eurosport, his eyes BB-pellet black and glassy. He breathes in snorting bursts through his nose, and he's close enough that he causes the still air in the car to circulate. Frozen, I stare at the nappy brown fur on his back. *Is it soft?* I manage to wonder. *Would he maul me if I touched him?* We stare at each other, frozen for minutes, when finally a red pickup truck pulls up and two very large women with cameras get out and call to the bison in Southern accents. He barely manages to lumber toward them, and I whisper-yell to Josh, "Start the car. Go!" And he does.

We laugh for the next several miles, breathless, hiccupy laughing, until we're out of Yellowstone and back on the highway. Elvis blaring, highway wind whooshing, conversation over. Nothing like a two-ton prairie animal to spoil the mood.

. . .

I got a letter from Ethan. I practically jumped when I found it in the mailbox. That's why I wouldn't give him my email. Gavin knows all my passwords. I thought snail mail would be safer. But I'm afraid someone is going to find this letter. I hid it under my bed, but that wasn't hidden enough. I wanted so bad to be able to read it over and over, but what would happen if Gavin found it? What would he do? Would he only be mad? Or would he be a little jealous? Like that one time I said I thought Johnny Depp was cute. He sulked for a week. It was almost sweet. I don't want to hurt him again. So I cram the letter down the garbage disposal with leftover baked beans.

CHAPTER EIGHTEEN

Our route to Portland can either take us through Montana and Washington or down through Idaho and Oregon. I'm partial to the Montana route, if only because it will take us through a city called Butte, which I suspect is supposed to rhyme with *cute* but is asking for *butt*. Josh, on the other hand, loves potatoes, so we head to Idaho. As if the state is just covered with Tater Tots. To challenge my cynicism, what should be our first stop but a giant potato photo op outside the (overkill!) Spud Drive In (easily located by the numerous potato-covered billboards). The giant potato turns out to be a big ol' faker, with no actual potato content, although it's lifelike enough. Perched on the back of a flatbed truck, the potato is, naturally, paired with an American flag.

I pull out my cell phone, which has been on and dying since Yellowstone, to take a picture. No message from Penny or Ethan yet, and no answer when I tried the number again.

"We're gonna lose the cell soon," I tell Josh, looking at the thin, red battery line.

"Maybe we can find one of those lighter chargers," he suggests.

"Out here? Not bloody likely. Unless it's potato powered." I shut the phone off to conserve batteries for when we're closer to Portland.

Our next stop is almost the town of Rigby, whose signs declare is the birthplace of television, but I'm feeling the tug of the quest and don't want to get sidetracked again. Besides, what exactly would there be to look at? A huge fake TV, with requisite American flag? Maybe it's made of potatoes. Idaho sure has me making potatoey jokes. That doesn't sound as good as corny did. Or cheesy, for that matter.

My mind rolling with potatoes, I soon decide that there's no more room for stops in Idaho. If we drive all night, we could make it to Portland by tomorrow morning. I drag my pen along the map of the Northwest, when I hit a most obvious snag. And it's not in the directions. "Josh . . . ," I say with a hint of whine.

"Lil . . . ," he mimics.

"How are we going to find Penny once we get to Portland?" I say this slowly, recognizing how I missed out on that opportunity in Deadwood.

"You have no idea at all where she is?" Josh quickly

turns his head to look at me, then back on the road. I detect a slight bit of annoyance, which only annoys me back. We wouldn't have Josh's journey of avoidance without Penny as the catalyst.

"Have you not been listening? I knew she was going to Portland to be with a guy named Ethan. That should narrow it down a bit, shouldn't it?" I waver between snark and panic.

"What about your phone? She called you from somewhere in Portland, right? So the number's on your phone."

"But we don't have much battery power. What if I turn it on, and there's no reception, and that wastes all the power? Or what if when I finally do turn it on, the battery's already completely dead?" The wavering is over; I'm hysterical that our spontaneity in leaving and lack of a plan have screwed our chances of quest success.

"I think you should definitely wait to call her until we're in Portland. Leave the phone off until then. If we try to call her now and the phone dies, we won't even have a phone number to not be able to find her with. Don't worry. It'll all work its way out." Josh calmingly puts his hand on my knee.

"OK," I breathe. "We wait until Portland," I agree. Even if I don't quite believe it.

We pass the long drive from the giant potato to Craters of the Moon National Monument (which we determine is

156

too cool-sounding to pass up) by calling out funny town names. "Irwin!" "Ririe!" "Rigby!" "Chubbuck!" But then we decide that none of them (except Chubbuck, of course) are all that funny. We make a turn at my favorite, Rupert (this state has an obvious love for British male names. Or maybe a bunch of British dudes named all the towns after themselves), and head to Craters of the Moon. I guess I'm hoping for a real live version of the FantaSuite hotel room, but with the sun shining brightly and tourists with ugly orange backpacks surrounding us, there's nothing much moon-like about it. The ground is black and ashy, craggy in some parts from lava. I guess that's the moon deal.

"They could have at least put in a fake alien head popping out from behind a rock or something," I note.

"Or a real one," Josh adds. "Next trip we'll go to Roswell, New Mexico, Area Fifty-One—the whole alien shebang." He puts his arm around me reassuringly.

"Next trip?" I ask.

"Yeah. Next road trip," he says as though stating a fact.

Is he just being Josh, making up fake plans for a fantastical future, or is another road trip, another summer, a possibility? I'm warmed by the idea, so we spend the next long leg of our loud highway journey yelling out names of places we want to see.

"The Grand Canyon!"

"The Alamo!"

"The basement of the Alamo!"

"There's no basement in the Alamo!" I yell, acknowl-edging the nod to *Pee Wee's Big Adventure*.

Josh allows me to take the wheel around Twin Falls, Idaho. I've only driven his car a few times, when he's needed both hands to record ambient sounds with a portable microphone to add to some of his music. But tonight, I drive because it's time I take control of the journey. And I don't want an overtired Josh to crash when we're this close to our destination. Before we get back on the highway, we stop for our second "Authentic Idahoan Meal," according to Josh.

"How is McDonald's authentic Idahoan?" I ask.

"Duh. Where do you think they get their fries?"

"Probably not from real potatoes, if they're anything like the burgers," I guess.

"Stop crapping all over my potato fantasies."

We drive, and Josh naps in the backseat as I navigate through Idaho country. Mountains peak into blue sky in every direction. I sing along with Elvis and know every guitar pluck and jangle by heart. When this trip is over I'm either going to build a memorial to this tape or burn it. Who knows? Maybe it will melt itself from exhaustion.

With Josh still asleep, I pass through Boise and then over into Oregon, celebrating the new state by myself. Not nearly as ceremonious as when done in tandem. By eleven o'clock, my heavy eyelids are ready to pull over. Josh lounges in the backseat, awake, and leans over my shoulder to whisper in my ear, "I'll take it from here. We'll be in Portland by daybreak."

His whisper inspires me. "No," I say. "Why don't we stop somewhere and stay the night? We don't even know where we're going once we get to Portland. You can't really call someone at daybreak." Although that's about when this whole thing started, isn't it?

Josh's head remains near my shoulder until we pull off the highway into a town called Pendleton. Appealingly homespun signs lead to the Rugged Mountain Lodge, several miles down the road, but I'm leaning toward the Motel 6 in plain sight. I pull into the parking lot. "We can't stop at a Motel Six when a Rugged Mountain Lodge is nearly in our grasp. I mean—Rugged. Mountain. Lodge," Josh enthuses. My head nods heavily, so Josh exits the backseat and slides me over just enough to fit into the driver's seat. I rest my head on his shoulder as he wraps his arm over mine.

We drive for another ten minutes until we spot a woodsy sign. It turns out the Rugged Mountain Lodge isn't a lodge at all, nor is it as rustic as it sounds. It is a bed-and-breakfast of the maximum quaint variety.

"Are we allowed to get here this late?" I yawn while we stand poised at the door. Bed-and-breakfasts have rules about comings and goings, I think. A doorbell with a sign reads, WELCOME, WEARY TRAVELERS.

"You're weary, aren't you?" Josh asks, and he rings the bell.

I expect a gaggle of roosters to crow and dogs to bark, to hear a man trip over the animals and yell, "Dagnabbit!" But instead, a woman of around forty in a fluffy bathrobe, her blond hair high in a ponytail, answers the door with a squinty smile.

"Sorry to be arriving so late. We've been on the road all day," Josh explains to the woman with his polite charm. I quickly swipe away the image of Josh in Cougartown.

The woman, whom I shall call "Hattie" because that sounds bed-and-breakfast, looks at us with her head cocked to one side, as if she's sizing up two teenagers at a bed-and-breakfast. There's a glint in her eye. Of recognition perhaps? Of days gone by when she took a road trip expecting some sort of clarity? Or maybe she just needs the business. "Oh, not a problem. We're happy to have you. Come in." Hattie welcomes us into a foyer, heavy on the floral, and asks us to sign the guest registry. I'm comforted that there are other names listed. Just in case this isn't a real bed-and-breakfast, and she's luring people here to kill and stuff us, like in that Roald Dahl story about the landlady. Man, I'm tired. "Will that be one room or two?" Hattie inquires.

"One," Josh answers quickly.

"One bed or two?" Is she prying? Or are these standard guest questions?

"One," Josh answers even quicker.

My stomach twinges a happy twinge, even though it has

been disappointed before by Josh and his friendly closeness. Or his close friendness. Just point me to the bed.

Josh hands Hattie his credit card, and she runs it through a tiny machine hidden in a drawer with a dangling golden handle. When we're cleared, she rummages through a small cabinet. "Here's your key. Room Four. I'll be up shortly with complimentary tea and cookies." Hattie says this with a hint of obligation, looking tired.

"Don't worry about that," I say. "We can just wait for breakfast tomorrow."

"You sure?" We both nod. "Well then, good night. Pleasant dreams."

Josh and I find our room at the end of the hall. Inside we are overwhelmed with flowers, covering walls, chairs, and a canopy bed. I almost start sneezing. "If this were a FantaSuite, what do you think it would be called?" I whisper. The house is so silent, any noise we make might be intercepted by the other Mountain Logders.

"Floral Explosion?" Josh guesses.

"Or what about Death by Dandelion?" I suggest. Josh nods in agreement.

We tiptoe around, getting ready for bed. I change into a fresh T-shirt that reads, PROUD OF MY WISCONSCENT, take off my shorts, and climb into bed while Josh finishes up in the bathroom. I click off the lights.

"Whoa. Darkness," Josh announces as he exits the bathroom.

"Want me to turn on the light?" I ask.

"Nah. I'll adjust." I hear him taking off clothes, probably his T-shirt. Then more clothes. I'm guessing his shorts. That leaves his boxers. And me in my undies.

Josh slides into bed next to me, the sheets tucked so tightly I can't keep my feet perpendicular without my toes getting smushed. I roll onto my side to face him.

The only light in the room glows from the red numbers on the alarm clock and from underneath the door leading to the hallway. Not a heavy-duty door, like in a hotel, but a regular, thin house door. I can just make out Josh's face, so close to mine I can smell his recently rinsed toothpaste.

"Hi," he says. It always bothers me when people do this little exchange in movies and on TV. So cutesy and fake. And yet . . .

"Hi," I reply. The words always leading. And he kisses me. And I kiss him. And then I stop and turn onto my back.

"Don't stop now," Josh prods. My words. My rock.

"Why, Josh? Why now?" Now in this bed-and-breakfast. Now on our trip. In our lives.

"Don't you want to?" His whisper is defensive.

"Of course," I whisper back. "I mean, I did. I do. I don't know." He flips over onto his stomach, his face toward me. "What would this mean?" I need to know. In the past, in high school, when we were together every day, I always pictured us as boyfriend and girlfriend, cutest-couple-yearbook material. Or maybe a senior edition newspaper nod. But what are we now, in the limbo between high school and college, where my immediate future is scheduled and his is, just, somewhere else?

"It doesn't have to mean anything. Or it could mean something, if you want it to." He strokes the strands of hair that hang around my face, his guitar-rough fingertips brushing my cheek.

"What do *you* want?" I ask.

"I want right now," he whispers, and props himself up on his arm.

"I want right now, too," I decide. Josh kisses me, and I let him. And I kiss him back, and he lets me. Together. Here. Now.

· · ·

My arm hurts so bad. It hurts so bad and looks so purple yellow green that I have to wear the blackest, softest shirt I own. Long sleeves, even though it's spring and it's time to put the sleeves away. The school hasn't turned off the heat yet even though they waited until it was so cold in December to turn it on. But now it's too warm inside and out for sleeves. I hope my antiperspirant works. I don't want sweat rings. I don't want to have to wear a sweater in April. The crap part is that Gavin asks me why I'm wearing a sweater. Why don't I show off that tan I got at Disney World? Why does he think? Does he not remember? Maybe he doesn't. It's like he has two personalities sometimes. The one I love, I love so much it hurts. And the other one, just hurts.

CHAPTER NINETEEN

I fall asleep soon afterward, enveloped in the warmth and strength of Josh's arms. We're woken up the next morning by a light tap on the door, and Hattie's voice calling out, "Breakfast!"

Josh's lips are directly next to my ear, and he rasps, "We've done the bed part; now it's the breakfast's turn."

I grope around in the dark to find my clothes and pull them on. I crack the curtains a tad to let in the daylight, and I catch a glimpse of Josh getting dressed. Somehow this should feel different, I think.

I pat down my hair, and ask, "Do I look presentable?"

"Beautiful, as always," Josh says, although barely looking as he smooths his own hair. Does he mean it in a new way or like he always meant it? Is his head swarming with questions like mine is?

We groggily head downstairs for breakfast. We find the dining room just past the entry hall from last night. Inside are a long table covered with a sunny yellow tablecloth and small glass vases with wildflowers down the center. The room is surrounded by floor-to-ceiling windows, looking out at a yard overrun with greenery. The only other diners are a family of five—Mom, Dad, and three girls who appear to be different sizes of the same person wearing the same clothes: pink overalls. I marvel at the genetics.

Hattie greets us with a friendly and very awake "Welcome" and points us toward the homemade muffins, granola, and scones on the buffet. There is also coffee, tea, and juice, and Josh and I pile our floral plates with at least one of everything.

I sit down across from one of the pink girls, the tallest, and smile. She smiles back tenfold, and exhales an enthusiastic "Hi! I'm Mary Margaret, and this is my sister, Catherine Ann, and my other sister, Elizabeth Lynn." Catherine Ann and Elizabeth Lynn both wave spastically. I'm stuck on their multiple names. Middle names make sense to me, so that you don't have to pick just one name when you have a kid, but more than one first name? Do they have middle names, too? Or maybe those are their middle names, and they were, like, "What's the point of having middle names if we don't get to use them every day?"

"I'm Leo, and this is my wife, Ruth," the dad, not so young anymore but handsome in a dad sort of way, introduces himself and his wife. His teeth seem to sparkle and *ding* at me.

"How do you do?" Josh says, surprising me with his hysterical over-formality. "I'm Joshua, and this is Lillian." I nod hello, barely able to contain a guffaw at Josh's full name usage, and consider adding my middle name (Beth) for consistency but am too tempted by my warm blueberry muffin to bother. I split the muffin down the middle with my hands and spread butter into the center, melting it instantly.

"What brings a nice couple like you to Oregon?" Leo asks. His question could be construed as prying, but I think he's genuinely interested. Leo seems like a man who is interested in people. The way he looks at us when he speaks, the way he smiles at his children. Must be nice.

Josh leans toward sincerity and answers Leo, "On our way to visit a friend in Portland."

"Big city, Portland." Leo angles his head thoughtfully.

"Is it? We're from Chicago, so we're not too worried." I wonder what Josh thinks of Leo. Does he make him think about his own dad at all? Does he make him want to call home and tell him where he is?

"Chicago! The Windy City. I've heard good things." Leo genially sips his coffee. Ruth has yet to say anything, but involves herself in the conversation by turning her head, complete with pert, neat blond bob, toward each speaker. What could Josh think of Ruth? A mom in the present. Josh has never said a word to me about his mother except to say that he *won't* say a word about her. Can he really go through the rest of his life pretending that he doesn't have to deal with anything?

As if on cue, Catherine Ann blurts out, "Is he your boyfriend?" Mary Margaret tsks her tongue and looks at Catherine Ann, incredulous.

"Catherine Ann." Ruth finds her voice to scold, "Don't pry."

"No big deal," Josh answers to Ruth, then looks at Mary Margaret. "We're—"

"Good friends," I interrupt. I don't know how Josh would have completed that sentence, but I decide that I'd rather hear it coming from my mouth than his. He's had too much say in where we stand for too long.

I stab at a blueberry muffin with my fork, and it rolls off my plate onto the spotless floor. Catherine Ann dives under the table to grab it, then pops back up into her chair.

"Here." She beams and hands the floored blueberry to me across the table.

"Thanks," I say with just a hint of what-the-hell-do-you-want-me-to-do-with-this? in my voice. I tuck the blueberry under my plate and finish the meal in silence. No one notices, as the Model Family parental units begin their assault of never-ending stories of the Redwood Forest, the Grand Canyon, and the Hoover Dam. Josh and I finally convince them we need to be on our way, and get back on the road around ten a.m. I keep occupied by studying the map and figure we have four hours tops before we arrive somewhere in Portland. I turn my phone on, and even with the weak reception, a text message manages to buzz its way into my phone. Mom. Just checking in. I shut it off again.

I know technically I could call Penny from the B and B or even a pay phone. All I have to do is pull the number off the cell and make life a little easier. We're getting so close, though, that I don't feel the need to rush. And really, right now, Penny isn't the main perturbance in my mind. No, that one is right next to me in his junky car.

The drive to Portland is gorgeous and green, mountainous and lush. The air in the car smells like forest, and the sky is patched with clouds like the opening credits of *The Simpsons*. I attempt to yell to Josh over the rumbling car sound to check out the clouds, but after three "What's?" I wave my hand to indicate, "Forget it." Something's not sitting right with me, and I don't think it's the twelve muffins I pounded to avoid asking inappropriate questions about middle names to the Leo family. If what happened last night with Josh was what I always wanted to happen with Josh, why does it feel like nothing even happened? Is it because we're not in reality—driving through limbo, destination: our uncertain futures? Is it only real if it happened before we graduated from high school? When "Cutest Couple" meant something? Once that yearbook's printed, who else in the world really gives a crap? Does Josh ever really give a crap?

And I can't get my mind off Leo. Not in *that* way, but

there was something off about those girls for sure. How the mom didn't talk that much. The double names, like, I give you *two* names, so that you see how much control I have over who you *are*. Or not? My mom claims my dad wanted me to be named Ryan, boy or girl, after some tool on the Chicago Cubs from seven hundred years ago. The way I ended up with Lillian? My dad wasn't actually at the hospital when it was time to name me. No, he was at a Cubs game. Which is fine. Life was harder with him around than without him. But that doesn't mean it doesn't get to me a little when I see a dad who seems to care. Would it have been nice to have my dad at my high school graduation? Probably. Would it have been nice to at least get a card in the mail? Yes, it would. But I didn't. And here Josh sits, bunged that all his dad gave him for graduation was an ultimatum to get a real job or go to college. Oh, and that new drum kit. I can't help it. "Hey!" I yell so loudly that I sound more angry than just trying to make Josh hear me. And maybe I am.

"What?" he yells back, an answering note of anger in his voice. Or maybe that's just him trying to be loud, too.

"I'm going to turn on my phone," I say, toning down the yell when I decide to just roll up my window. The abrupt quiet on my right side makes my ear pop.

"Think you'll get any reception?" he asks, rolling up his own window so we can speak in civilized tones. What a novel idea.

"Maybe. I at least need to text my mom back. She says hello." Josh nods. "You want to call your dad?"

Though the windows are up, Josh answers with a head shake.

"Text him?"

Another head shake.

Even with his stubble and deliciously defined chest (the shirt came off about an hour into the drive), he looks like an obnoxious, spoiled kid shaking his head like that.

"Sorry I asked." I turn my head toward my window, already lowering it to let the welcome din back in.

We drive out of the more scenic views and into city views, announcing our arrival in Portland. If and when we find Penny, is that it? Quest over? And will connecting with Penny bring me back to high school, make what happened with Josh and me more real? Or will it finally get me past, over, and out into real life? Oddly, my answer comes in the form of a road sign. MILWAUKIE, it reads. Spelled wrong. Like home, like where we started, but not quite.

"Almost like we never left, huh?" Josh yells to me.

"I'd say we've actually gone pretty far," I muse, not so mad as before. Signs are signs sometimes.

"I wonder if it's like a *Twilight Zone* parallel-universe Milwaukee. Something not quite right about it. You can tell by the *i*."

"Definitely something not quite right about the *i*," I say, and can't help but smile a little. I bet Josh has no idea that I'm even thinking about last night. He's probably writing songs about blueberry muffins or something in his head. His beautiful, shirtless head. I decide to regain focus on why we're here. Or, at least, why we're supposed to be here.

We follow signs toward the city center, and I know it's time for the fateful cell-phone-power-on moment. Josh pulls into a parallel parking spot so I can hear—if there is anything *to* hear. I hold the power button down, and the phone lights up. The battery image flashes, indicating it's now or never to make the call. I flip through the call folder, received calls. I want to have more of a plan of what I'll say, but I'm already wasting time by having to sift through the folders to get to the numbers. I find the unfamiliar digits and will my thumb to hit Call. The phone on the other end rings. And rings. And rings again. I look over at Josh with a panicked head shake, and the rings turn into voicemail.

"Hi, this is Ethan. Leave me a message," Ethan's pleasant voice tells me. Do I leave another message? I'm not quick enough with the decisions today, but the message beeps anyway, forcing me to either hang up or speak. I manage to speak. "Hey, Ethan, this is Lillian Erlich again?" I'm speaking in question form, and I hate the wimpy sound of it. I shift gears and state, "She needs to call me. I'm in Portland, and I have to talk to her. My cell number is . . ." I leave the number, say thanks, and hang up. At that moment, my phone beeps the message, "Battery low," and the screen goes blank. You've got to be shitting me.

CHAPTER TWENTY

What's going on? You left a message?" Josh looks confused by the defeat on my face.

"The phone's dead," I say with a pout.

"We can go try and find a car charger. There's got to be a phone store around here somewhere." He scans the street vigorously, making a huge effort to prove he's making a huge effort. It's nice and all, but I can't help but feel like the phone death was a sign.

"What does it matter? She'll probably call back when the phone is dead and not leave a message."

"She's not that stupid. She'll leave a message and you'll call her back. Ain't no thang."

"I'll call her back, and then I'll have to leave a message, and then she'll call me back, and so on and so on and so on. It'll be a never-ending cycle of phone messages until we have to rent an apartment and find jobs in Portland because we can't get in touch with her and we can't go home because the FBI will be camped out on my doorstep and

Penny's mom will sell commemorative Penny plates on QVC and . . ." I'm delirious. The quest crushed. Stuck in limbo.

"Lillian." Josh leans toward me and puts one hand on each of my shoulders. He butts his forehead up against mine and says calmly, "It will be okay. The worse thing that can happen is we don't find her, you call home, and turn her in. You'll look like a hero, and life moves on."

"What's the best thing that could happen?" I ask, entranced by his closeness.

"We find her and make *her* turn herself in, thus ending our journey and ridding ourselves of the plague of Penny for good."

I guess that's the best, although it seems weird to have a "best" of anything include the word *plague*. And if he thinks she's such a plague, does that mean he thinks this road trip was a bad thing? Am I overthinking Josh's underthinking brain?

"I need coffee," I huff.

"That's my girl," he says, and kisses my forehead.

"You missed," I deadpan.

"Yeah, well, my aim's not so good today." He winks. I'd like to poke a stick in that winking eye.

We drive around for a few minutes until we spot a sign reading, VOODOO DOUGHNUT. "Doughnuts and voodoo?" Josh enthuses, "I'm sold!" It does sound good. And weird. As argumentative as I'm feeling, who can argue with that?

We enter through a red door, into a tiny grimy counter store with pinkish mood lighting and stacks of doughnut boxes everywhere. The crowd inside is hipster extreme and reeks of smoke and last night's pub crawl. The too-cool-to-be-nice character behind the counter exudes the right amount of service and snub. I feel stupid ordering some Voodoo Doughnuts (shaped like voodoo dolls, of course) and coffee to go. There are other quirky-cool options, like the Triple Chocolate Penetration and Butter Fingering, but I can only assume the cool counter character (say it fast three times) has snarky comments for pervy items on the menu (Or maybe not. Maybe he's too cool for snark. Either way, I'm not pushing it before my morning coffee).

We leave Voodoo Doughnut with our bag of dolls and coffee cups and decide to walk around and check out the city instead of enduring the hipsterosity. The day is nice, the air not too hot, sun shining but not too roasty. It feels like we're in another place, which, of course, we are. But sometimes when you fly places, it just feels like you never left home. Driving here exposes the differences: street signs shaped differently from ours, unique WALK and DON'T WALK buttons, and even foreign garbage cans. I can almost see why someone would choose to run away. Or at least get away. To experience the slight differences of everyday life. And the huge ones, too.

We wander the streets, not paying strict attention to how far or which direction. My dead phone weighs heavily in my pocket, so I pull it out and hand it to Josh. "Can you carry this? I don't need the reminder." I'd rather pretend for a few seconds that I'm just visiting. Just living life in a different place.

"Sure thing," Josh says and tucks the phone into the pocket of his shorts.

We get to an area near water, and I don't know enough about Portland to know if it's a river, a lake, or an ocean. I mean, I know Portland is near the ocean, but this could be anything. A tributary? I search my brain for watery words learned in elementary school. People are set up to sell their artsy-craftsy wares, while others, with clearly nothing better to do, sit on boxes, a hat out for spare change. One guy, a particularly grungy, bearded fella, attempts a tap dance to coax some money out of us as we walk by. Josh pulls out a dollar bill from his pocket and tosses it into the worn baseball cap the man presents as a finale to his performance. "At least he entertained us," Josh concedes.

A bridge connects our side of Portland to the other side, and we decide we might as well cross it. "We'll cross that bridge when we come to it." Josh chuckles. "And we've come to it."

"Yeah." I roll my eyes. The bridge itself isn't particularly lovely, mostly for cars, but the view is interesting and exposes numerous bridges connecting Portland on either side of us. I'd maybe take a picture if my phone worked. Dang. Thought I almost forgot.

The traffic on the bridge makes it too noisy to talk, and when we get to the other side, we hear a familiar sound.

"Skaters?" I ask.

"Sounds like it," Josh concurs, and we discover a skate park located near the base of the bridge. A group of young guys, and even a few girls, ride ramps and bowls most impressively. "I always wanted to be good at skating," Josh laments, stroking the road-trip stubble on his chin.

"I didn't even know you skated," I say.

"I never have, actually. I just wanted to be good at it." He gives me a wry smile.

"Oh. Well, then, I always wanted to be good at synchronized swimming."

"And are you?" Josh asks.

"Don't know. I've only done it by myself." I smirk.

We're smiling at each other, kind of dumbly, when I catch something written on an alley wall near the bridge. It strikes something familiar in me, so I walk toward it. When I get closer, I can't help but exhale, "No. Way." Then I call back to Josh, who hasn't moved, and yell, "No way!" I wave to him to follow me, and we walk into the alley. I stare at the brick wall in disbelief, where an exact replica of my spray-painted Badlands rock mantra stares me in the face: DON'T STOP NOW. "This is what it said on the rock! The rock where we kissed in the Badlands! It's the exact same thing!" I'm yelling like a loon, completely blown away by this discovery.

Josh is predictably underwhelmed. "Maybe the guy who painted it likes to travel," he suggests.

"Maybe," I say, annoyed at his nonchalance. "And maybe it's a sign."

"That we should kiss again?" Josh waggles his eyebrows at me, but I'm not so sure. I study Josh's face. I remember how he felt, so close to me as I slept in his arms. The way his lips pressed against my shoulders, my neck, my lips. My eyes feel heavy, and I'm taken in as he leans into me with a soft kiss. His lips taste like doughnut and coffee. I kiss him for a moment, a minute, and then I hold him away from me, my hand on his chest.

"No," I tell him. About the kiss. About the sign. "'Don't stop now' means we have to keep going. To find Penny. To complete the quest." I need Josh to understand that there are other things in my world besides him. As much as my heart wants to stay on this bridge, this close to Josh, indefinitely.

He shrugs off my dismissal and agrees in mellow Josh fashion, "Why not?"

We watch a few guys circle one another on the wavy skate landscape. While I'm scanning the skaters to find a friendly face, an insanely good-looking bleached-blond guy with icy blue eyes rolls past us in what feels like slow motion. We make eye contact, and my face gets involuntarily hot. I think about asking him, or any of them, if they know Ethan or have seen Penny, but that seems so random. So Josh and I keep moving.

"I like the idea of keeping to the water," I say.

"'Keeping to the water?' With your mare named Lucy?" Josh chides.

"What? What does that even mean?"

"What does 'keeping to the water' mean?"

"It means that we walk along the water. Like when you're in Chicago, and you know what direction you're headed if you know where Lake Michigan is."

"But I never got that. Because, like, if I don't know where I am, how the hell am I going to know where the lake is? Unless I'm standing right in it."

"Good point. But if we don't remember where the water is, then we don't find the Eurosport when we walk back. So let's just go either this way"—I point to what I think is north—"or this way," which I think is south.

"Flip a coin?" Josh asks, and I nod. He pulls a quarter from his pocket and flicks it perfectly with his thumb. The coin spins in the air and lands on the concrete, rolling into a sewer grate. "You didn't call it," Josh presses.

"Would you have been able to read it if I did?"

"True enough. Take two." Josh pulls a penny out of his pocket. "I'm going penny this time. Just in case, you know, it falls into the abyss again." Flick. Fall. Roll. Grate. "Dude, you still didn't call it."

"Dude, it fell through a hole again. This doesn't really bode well for the future of this journey, does it?"

"Will you stop looking for things to mean other things?

180

Sometimes coins just fall down holes. That doesn't mean the world is going to end or you're going to grow a beard or anything."

"What?"

"I just mean that you make such a big deal out of everything. Life doesn't have to be so complicated." He looks at me as if what he's saying is the god's honest truth. That I should just accept it. But I'm tired of accepting things from Josh.

"Life doesn't have to be so complicated?" I ask him, trying to hold it together so I can make a point instead of start crying out of frustration. "Tell that to Penny, who had to fake her own kidnapping to get away from something, or someone, that made her paranoid enough to do such a crazy-ass thing. Tell that to my mom, who had to raise me while trying to deal with the fact that her husband was a selfish bastard who made our lives hell until he decided to just leave. Tell that to your dad, whose idea of love is giving you his credit card and access to his liquor cabinet." Josh is about to say something, to defend himself maybe, to tell me off, but I keep going. "Tell that to me, who has to deal with all of these people, plus one who has made my life nothing but complicated since the moment I laid eyes on his perfect face."

I run out of steam but manage to hold my eyes on Josh's face. He doesn't look so comfy, as relaxed as he usually does. His lips are pursed, the corners of his mouth tipped downward. He pulls his dick shades out of his back pocket and puts them on, so now what I see is my fake red hair and distorted face reflected back at me.

"That's exactly what I mean," I tell him, still trying to keep what I think is his gaze but really might just be mine.

"What—," Josh starts, but can't find the right words. He kicks at the ground with the peeling rubber from his Chucks.

"I mean that by pretending that nothing is going on between you and me, and everything else, *that* complicates things."

"Kind of harsh, Lil," Josh mutters.

"And kind of true, Josh. I know some of it is my fault. I could have just given up on liking you and been totally perfectly fine with us just being friends. But you kind of made that hard. Friends don't hold hands and lean against each other and, you know, *sleep together*? Complicated, Josh. Complicated."

"Complicated?" Josh repeats again for humorous emphasis.

"That doesn't even sound like a real word anymore, does it?" I half laugh, not wanting Josh to miss the truth in what I said.

"You know, my dad's not that bad," Josh says quietly.

"I know. But then why don't you want to call him?"

"'Cause I'm pissed, I guess, that he can be so cool for my whole life up until now, and then it's, like, 'Be a grown-up. Get a job. Turn into The Man I always wanted you to be.' You can't just drop that on someone and expect them to be into it, you know?"

"I think your dad actually expects something of you, Josh. That's a good thing. He thinks you're capable of more than just mooching."

"I'm not mooching! He's my dad. I was his kid until this whole high school graduation thing. Dads pay for their kids to do stuff."

"Some of them," I remind him.

"Well, some moms don't send their kids texts every five minutes to tell them they love them."

"It's not every five minutes. But, yeah, some moms suck, too." We stand in the industrial quiet of the concrete street. "What happened with your mom, Josh?"

I expect nothing from him. Maybe a joke, or something equally inappropriate or dismissive. But Josh talks. "My dad said she loved me. That she still loves me because moms love their kids. That it's his fault, and I should blame him one hundred percent. He cheated on her with her best friend. She told him that he broke her. That she lost both her best friends because of him. I was two. Everyone said that I looked just like my dad. That's what he said. Same hair, when he had it"—Josh tries to laugh—"same dark eyes. Same laugh. I bet she couldn't stand the sight of me. That's gotta be why she left me with him. Why she never came back."

"I'm so sorry, Josh," I say, hating that it's all I can come up with.

He shrugs. "I don't want to ever make you feel like that, Lil."

I don't know if he means cheated or abandoned or blamed. What I do finally understand is why he can't decide whether it's safe to love somebody.

I take Josh's hand in mine. "You won't, Josh. No matter what happens, I know you won't."

Josh lifts my hand to his mouth and kisses it softly. I bring his hand to my mouth and kiss it, too. We stand for a minute, me looking into my own reflection, him looking, I think, back at me.

Josh digs his free hand into his pocket. "Last penny," he says.

"Ha. Last *Penny*, get it?"

"Ah, yes, I remembered we were here for some reason. Shall I flip?"

"Why don't we move over a little this time. So we don't lose the penny. That way, maybe we can find the Penny."

Josh and I hold tight to each other's hands and move into the street. "Heads is north, tails is south," he says. Josh flips the coin, and this time I remember to call "heads." "Why did you call it? Heads is already north. It's not like you win anything."

"Shut up," I tell him.

We watch the coin as it flies up into the air and lands

with a roll on the street. Holding hands, we clumsily follow it and will it not to stop near a sewer grate. Finally, the penny tips onto a yellow stripe in the road.

"Yahtzee!" Josh yells.

"Um, I believe that's tails."

"Southbound we go," Josh declares. He bends down to retrieve the penny, but I stop him.

"It's bad luck to pick up a penny when it's on tails."

"Really? Where'd you hear that?"

"I don't know. Same place I learned it's bad luck to put shoes on beds."

"So, you mean the School of Stupid Superstitions?"

"Say that five times fast," I tell Josh. And he does. Hand in hand, as we walk south, sans penny.

* * *

Ethan. I didn't tell Lillian that we were just friends. That we hung out at the pool all day and I talked and talked about Gavin. Ethan told me about his ex and the debate team and his plans for college and to become a famous screenwriter. I told Lil that he was sweet and romantic. Which I bet he is. But not with me. 'Cause who'd be romantic with a girl who is so in love with someone that it consumes her?

CHAPTER TWENTY-ONE

outh takes us down a lovely walkway called the Eastbank Esplanade, which sounds so old-fashioned and fancy but is actually a nice bike path. Part of me believes that if we just keep walking, we'll run into Penny. The rest of me thinks I'm an idiot and that I will have to face facts and call the police soon enough. For right now, the sun is shining, my hand is only a tad sweaty from all of the Josh holding, and my head is just a bit clearer than it was when this whole trip started.

We walk until the esplanade comes to an end, and farther than that toward signs leading to the Oregon Museum of Science and Industry. "I wonder how much it's like the Chicago Museum of Science and Industry," I consider.

"Yeah, like do they have a weird miniature castle, filled with expensive crap some crazy person collected throughout their life?" Josh asks.

"Or that freaky coal mine, where it's so dark and you're

always afraid there's going to be a dead bird, signifying a gas leak."

"Nevermind the fact that you're just technically underneath a museum."

"Technically."

We reminisce about school field trips and museum memories and decide to check out the OMSI as long as we're there. When we walk into the lobby, however, we both realize that the museum could take an entire day to explore, and it's not far from closing time.

"Let's just do one of their special exhibits, and then we can run through the rest of the museum. We've seen all this stuff anyway in Chicago." I look up at the weird dinosaurs flying above me. "What are dinosaurs doing here? Shouldn't they be their history museum?" I'm thinking of Chicago's Field Museum, where the dinosaurs live.

"Dinosaurs are sort of sciencey, aren't they?"

"Scientifically historic," I argue.

"Historically scientific?"

"Whatever. What do you want to see?" The pricing board offers a special exhibit on space, which seems too generic. But there's a sign that catches my eye. "Laser light shows?"

"Check out the list: Pink Floyd, Rush, Michael Jackson!"

"We have to do this."

When we approach the cashier, we're sadly informed

that the main musical light shows aren't held until evening, so we settle on tickets for a light show titled "Laser
Space Odyssey," which sounds almost as sweet, promising
"Brilliant laser imagery choreographed to music ranging
from rock to classical."

We have about a half hour to kill before the show
starts, so we stop by the food court and pick up some hot
dogs. Josh orders his with ketchup (Chicago-style blas-
phemy), and I ask for mine with pickles and mustard. We
sit on a bench in the museum and watch people walk by.
"Do you think they know we're from out of town?" I ask.

"It's a museum. Probably a lot of people are from out
of town."

I agree and bite off a hunk of hot dog. Josh watches me
with a smirk. "What?" I demand, mouth full of food.

"You look pretty sexy eating that hot dog." Josh grins.

"Perv," I say.

"Especially with that mustard all over your chin." Josh
laughs and wipes it off with the side of his hand.

When we finish eating, we get in line for the laser show.
The room we enter is circular, with rows of reclining
seats. I'm surprised at how crowded the place is on a week-
day, but then I remember we're not the only people in the
world who are out of school. We find two seats in the front
row, and I nestle into mine, waiting for the ceiling pro-
gram to begin.

"You know," Josh leans over and whispers in my ear,

189

"I think we're mandated by the state of Oregon to make out during a laser light show."

I consider this. "Have you been studying state constitutions again?"

Josh nods in a little-kiddish way.

The lights dim, the music blares, and for the next half hour, Josh and I *are* the only people in the world.

After the laser show, I start to get anxious. Whether or not we actually find Penny, we have to at least do something. Our car is miles away, our home is thousands of miles away, and the police and FBI, not to mention Penny's worried parents, still need information.

"I think we should buy a car charger for the phone," I tell Josh.

"Guess so. We'll probably pass a store on the way back to the car."

Reluctantly, we leave the OMSI without seeing anything but the laser show, and that we didn't even really see.

We take the bike path north this time, back toward where we came. About a half hour later, we end up near the skate park again, signifying the bridge to return us to our car. The same familiar scraping and rolling sounds greet us, and we both slow down to watch some of the tricks the skaters are attempting on the ramp. As if we never left, the exact same gorgeous blond-haired, blue-eyed skater rolls by. This time, he rolls up to us and flips his board with his foot into his hands. "Can I help you guys?"

I'm struck silent by his directness of question and gaze. Can he help us? I look at Josh, and he looks at the skater with suspicion. But we're here and have nothing else to go on, so I ask, "Do you know a guy named Ethan?"

The skater surprises me by answering, "Maybe." But then he adds, "And maybe I know a couple guys named Ethan. One's blond with dreads, one's got a shaved head. Take your pick."

"I would, but I've never actually seen the guy." So helpful.

"OK. What's his last name?" The skater tips his head to the side in a pensive manner. I'm sure Penny told me his last name, or maybe I saw it on one of his letters, but at the moment, I go blank.

"Don't know that either," I say, trying to laugh at the absurdity.

"So you don't know what he looks like, you don't know his last name. What do you know?" This guy could be a jerk, but he actually seems genuinely like he's trying to help. And he's so not bad to look at. *Focus.*

"I know he's hanging out with my friend Penny."

"Do you know what *she* looks like?" he asks.

Ha. "I do. In fact . . ." That's when I remember the

191

picture of Josh and me, with the lurking Penny in the background, in my wallet. I pull it out, and Josh gives me a questioning look, like, *why* do you have that in your wallet? I answer his look: "Now we have a picture to show people. Of Penny." He peers at the picture.

"I didn't even realize she was in it."

Skater Boy looks at the photo. "That's a nice picture of you guys."

"Thanks. I think so, too." I wonder if he's referring to us looking good together or just us looking good, me specifically. "That's Penny in the back. With the cup."

Skater Boy stares at the picture for several long seconds, then puts up his pointer finger and says, "Hold." He walks over to a group of girls sitting on the side of a ramp, watching and hooting at the guys skating, and shows them the picture. They glance at it, then turn their eyes on me and Josh. Skater Boy points to the picture, assumingly guiding their eyes to Penny. Most of the girls shake their heads, but I note that one has a look of recognition. She then nods her head slowly and says something to him. Skater Boy returns, and I watch the group of girls smile toward us, toward Josh. Not unusual, but what is unusual is that for the first time I feel like I actually have a one up on all the other girls. And I know I'm *not* just one of the other girls to Josh.

Skater Boy rolls on over (I do love a skater's leany posture), flips up his board again, and says, "Reggie thinks she's seen her with a friend of her cousin's. Could be this Ethan you so eloquently described."

I smirk at this adorable skater under a viaduct thousands of miles from home. Does Josh feel my familiar twinge of jealously? Or does he, too, know things are different? Skater Boy smirks back. Slightly flustered, I ask, "Do they know where I might find this faceless cousin-friend?"

"Reg thinks he might work at Powell's."

"What's that?"

"It's a giant bookstore. You never heard of it?"

"We're not from around here," Josh cuts in. I detect a note of non-Joshness in his voice. Is he being territorial?

"Head west on the Burnside Bridge," he points up. "It's about a mile, a mile and a half west."

"Which way is west?" I ask. Skater Boy takes his skateboard in both hands and uses it to direct us toward west, like one of those guys on an airport runway who wears giant headphones.

"Good luck. Hope you find your friend. Stop back and let us know if you're in the area again."

"Maybe we will." I blink slowly.

"Thanks, man." Josh offers his hand to Skater Boy to shake.

"The name's Owen," Skater Boy says.

"Josh. And this is Lillian."

"Josh." Owen nods. "Lillian," Owen takes my hand to

shake, but leans forward and kisses it with a faux debonair manner. Then he hops oh-so-casually onto his skateboard and skims along a ramp. Josh takes hold of my Owen-kissed hand, not aggressively, but firmly, and we head back to the bridge, back in the direction we came, on our way to the bookstore and our clue.

* * *

Lillian was picking me up to go to dinner with her and her friends. They are still only her friends. But she is my friend, and that is enough. I didn't talk much at dinner, but I thought a lot. I thought about my idea for a plan. I think it could work. Ethan said in one of his letters, there have been many, that he wants to see me. Maybe not in that way, but he wants to see me. I could go to him. Even after seeing me in a bikini and hearing my stories. Even though I haven't written him back more than a couple times in case I got caught on the way to the post office with a letter to him in my hand. Lillian helped me mail the last one, though. She even addressed it in her own handwriting, just in case. It's the letter where I tell him I'm coming. I hope he's OK with it. I never gave him my phone number, just in case he actually called. Let's hope he's OK with it. Lillian didn't ask what or why. She just sent the letter. She's easy like that. Which is good, since I'm going to need her help.

CHAPTER TWENTY-TWO

The walk over the bridge is noisy and rumbly, but it feels on purpose this time. Powell's, a bookstore, possibly Ethan's place of employment, could be the clue we need to find Penny. What else do we have? Sure, we could charge the phone and wait for a call or call again, but that would mean we'd either have to sit in a café while it charged or drive around while it charged. And neither of those options feels very productive. The fact that maybe we actually have a lead, just from asking one person, in a whole huge city, has me jazzed. Maybe I should consider a career in detective work if writing doesn't work out. Or maybe I could write crime novels.

As we walk, I point to random signs, pieces of garbage, people on the street—anything that seems cluelike. Josh dismisses the idea that a scrap of paper with the letter *P* on it could be a sign that we're on the right track to find Penny. "Penny starts with *P*, you know," I point out.

"Yeah. I know." He pats me on the head condescendingly.

"Naysayer," I accuse. "You'll be sorry when I'm right."

"Why would I be sorry if you're right? You crazy."

"Shut up." We walk a ways in silence, not really angry, but more absorbing this new city. People are out and about, and it's fun to look around and think about everyone going to work or going about their daily routines, while here we are in the middle of a quest.

By the time we reach Powell's, Josh and I are starving. "Probe first. Eat second."

"Who said anything about probing?" Josh looks at me, grossed out.

"You know what I mean. We're going to probe the bookstore. For info. For clues. For leads."

"I think I probe better on a full stomach."

"And how would you know how you probe better if you haven't probed prior to today?"

"Let's just get the probing underway, shall we?"

Powell's really is huge—an entire city block long. The outside has a marquee, like an old movie theater, announcing an upcoming book's release. Inside, the store is massive, with color-coded room after room of new and used books, coexisting. Such a cool idea for a bookstore. However, when you are searching for someone in a block-long bookstore, it's somewhat like that needle-in-a-haystack

197

metaphor. We pass through the green room, the blue room, the gold room, the coffee room, the orange room, and up into the red, purple, and pearl rooms, searching for, well, I'm not sure. Did I expect Penny to be sitting atop a pile of bestsellers? Pop out from behind a stack of vampire novels? Peek out from the puppet-show curtain in the kids' room? Once we're back on the bottom floor in the gold room for the second time, I stop abruptly and Josh smacks into me.

"Why'd you stop?" he asks.

"We're not getting anywhere," I puff.

"Seems to me like we're getting somewhere," Josh says, close enough to wrap his arms around me and lean his head on my shoulder.

"Not now, dear, we have a mission. I'm just going to ask someone who works here if they know an Ethan."

"You do that. I'll wait here." Josh plunks himself down into a comfy chair and pulls an art book off a shelf with an artistically (but really, not so much) naked woman on the cover. Darling.

I leave Josh to his porn and approach an older man at an information desk. He wears glasses on a beaded chain perched on the tip of his nose, a bookstore cliché in the flesh. He does not look up from the catalog he reads, either because he doesn't notice I'm here or doesn't think I look distinguished enough to break his concentration. Do I tap my fingers? Clear my throat? I opt for picking up a nearby tale of nautical fiction (and yes, they do have a section dedicated to that) and plop it lightly on the counter. No response. I pick up the sea shanty and drop it higher and harder onto the counter. Still nothing. I sigh loudly and dramatically, but this catalog must be a literary delight because the old man and the specs aren't budging. Maybe he's a statue, I think for a skeptical moment, and then I take my book of ships and fish and bang it on the counter with a *whump*! Old Man Withers looks up. "Yes?" Is he seriously annoyed that I interrupted his catalog time?

"The sign above you says 'information.' Am I correct in assuming that I may ask you a question?" I don't mean to be a whippersnapper, but *come on*. I get more respect from my gym teacher on days when I claim to have my period so I don't have to run. And that's for the third time in one month.

"Yes?" Now he just sounds like a confused old man, and I feel guilty for being sassy.

"Um, I was wondering if you could tell me if a guy named Ethan works here."

"Kent?" he repeats.

"Ethan," I correct.

"Ethan?"

"Ethan."

Please don't ask me again.

Big sigh.

Look at the ceiling.

Bigger sigh.

"Full or part time?" he asks.

"I'm not sure," I say. I was just hoping, with the INFORMATION label, that this desk might have all the answers. Because I am still relatively answer free.

"I don't know the names of a lot of the part-timers, particularly if they work in the evening. I'll have to go and check with someone else. Can you wait here?" It seems that once the man has revved up his engine, he moves at a decent clip. I watch him walk into another room and wonder if he'll be able to find his way back to me with the information. Not because he's old, but because there are so many things to distract him. The simple question of "full or part time?" has me wondering if my sighting of the "Don't Stop Now" mantra was as much of a sign as that random paper *P*.

I look over at Josh, who now has his "art" book turned sideways, and I turn away, grossed out by the imagery. I wonder what kind of books Skater Boy Owen is into. Manga? Or high fantasy? Maybe old lady murder mysteries.

I'm shaken out of my bizarre book selection process for Owen when the grunchy man returns to his post. This time I notice his name tag, SOL, and the earring in his right ear. I make a mental note of him for a possible future book character.

"Here's what I've got for you," he says, and he hands me a scrap of paper that reads, "Friday 7–close, Monday 7–close, Thursday 7–close."

"This is someone's schedule," I say, assuming he gave me the wrong piece of paper.

Big sigh.

"That is correct. *Ethan's* schedule."

"Oh! So Ethan does work here. And this is his schedule." I marvel at what could be a huge bit of luck, if it weren't for the fact that this could really just be anyone named Ethan. Or not? There was that possible skater connection. I look over the schedule again. "Is that this coming Friday?" I ask Sol.

He nods and croaks, "Mmmhmm."

"So that's still two days away."

"That is correct. Such a bright young lady."

I smile at him quickly and sarcastically. "I need to see him before then. Is there any way I could get his phone number from you?"

"Sorry, sweetie, but that's against our policy."

"You guys have a policy about giving out employee phone numbers? Really?"

"How do we know what you'd use it for? You could be a stalker. Or a jealous ex. Or a serial killer. One never knows." Sol smiles in a disturbingly fake manner.

"No. One doesn't, does one?" I'm starting to wonder if Sol would have told me had I just been a tad nicer, but the look on his face is resolute. At least I think it is. Hard to tell under all those wrinkles. "Well, thank you anyway."

I start to walk away when he asks, "Would you like to leave a note?"

I consider it but decide that if he won't be here for two days anyway, I have those two days to decide whether or not to write the note. I shake my head no to Sol.

Discouraged, I force myself over to Josh with the hopes that he has moved on to literature less graphic. Thankfully he has, although the title, *Lucky Lydia*, suggests pervier content might be inside. At least there aren't any pictures. That I can see. It must be engrossing enough because he doesn't notice me. What's with men not noticing me at this bookstore? I seemed to get noticed pretty quickly at the skate park. . . . I kick Josh's shoe harder than intended, and he jumps as if caught doing something he shouldn't. Which he is, in my opinion. What is it that gives guys the right to look at skanky women whenever they want? Oh, right, it's the fact that skanky women are everywhere, à la Victoria's Secret whorehouse window displays, so why would men think any differently? Really, men are just poor, innocent victims of our advertising media. I kick Josh's shoe again, and he gives me a what-the-hell? look. I glance down at the book he holds, and he gives an embarrassed shrug, then a nod of acknowledgment.

"Any leads, detective?" he asks, putting the book down and pushing himself out of the chair.

"Sort of, but nothing helpful. Someone named Ethan does indeed work here, but not for another two days. I mean, we could just hang around Portland, but what if it's not even him? And what if it is, but we can't find him in this giant bookstore? Or what if he's in the business of protecting Penny, too, and he lies to me just like I've been lying to the FBI? Hopeless."

"Hopeless? We have landed in a city, population: um, something million, and in less than a day you have found three people who know someone named Ethan. Pretty good."

"Three people who know *someone* named Ethan? How is that anything? That's nothing! That's a joke! That's me being pathetic and pretending there is something when there is obviously nothing." I pause. Pretending there's something when there is obviously nothing. That's what I was doing with Josh for the last four years. But then it turns out that there is something. That there was something there all along. And I saw it. And now he sees it. Maybe you just have to believe in something really hard to find it. Even when it's right in front of you. Maybe I thought Penny needed my help, but she knew how to help herself all along. "Huh," I say.

"Huh?" Josh looks confused.

"Yeah. Huh. I think I've figured something out."

"You know where to find Penny?"

"No. But, I think I might be done trying to help her. I don't even think she needs my help. I think she knew what she was doing when she left home. She was smart enough to fake a kidnapping and confuse her parents, the police, and the FBI. Not to mention us . . ."

"Which is more impressive than the three of those put together," Josh interjects.

"Most definitely. We have clues. And leads. And when we buy that phone charger, we'll have her contact info. Then, I can call her, tell her I know she's OK, that she needs to call her parents and the police and straighten this whole thing out. She is totally capable and strong enough to do it. I mean, she managed to come out here all by herself, didn't she? Even if it was in the most jacked-up, round-about way imaginable."

"I think it would have been more jacked-up if it involved circus clowns."

"Yeah, I guess you're right. Clowns would have been the cherry on top of the crazy cake."

"Speaking of crazy cake—can we get something to eat now?"

I take Josh's hand, and we head out to find food and a cell phone charger. And hopefully no circus clowns.

• • •

I got the letter. I threw up because I was so nervous, and then I flushed it down the toilet with my puke. But the toilet clogged, and I had to plunge it. Mom came around the bathroom to ask what was happening. I told her nothing, that I had a big lunch, and it was fine. Just using the plunger. She asked if I needed help. I yelled no, and that made her mad and she walked away. The puke and the letter went down finally, and I sat on the lid. I can't believe it's going to work. It's going to happen. I'm going to do it. Portland, here I come. I hope this bruise on my stomach goes away before I get there.

CHAPTER TWENTY-THREE

Across the street from Powell's is Rocco's Pizza, where Josh orders a whole pepperoni pizza instead of just shelling out for two slices. He whips out the credit card, and adds two Cokes to the bill. I plop down at a small table by the window so we can look out on the street.

"You know, slices would have been fine," I tell Josh when he joins me, hands full of napkins and our drinks.

"I know. But the whole pizza costs more." Josh taps his straw on the table to remove the paper wrapper.

"And that's a good thing?"

"I'm going to burn out this credit card until my dad cuts me off."

"Josh, I don't think your dad's going to cut you off. He just wants you to be more responsible."

"I'm responsible," he defends himself.

"Really? Like, by not telling your dad that you left town? By using his credit card to pay for hotel rooms? Food? A cheese-shirt wardrobe?"

"You didn't seem to mind."

"True, but that's not the point, is it?"

Josh curls his straw wrapper into a ball on the table. "The bite is that he won't even notice, Lil. I could buy a football team, not that I would, and he would just write the check and seal the envelope. He's too busy with his twelve-year-old girlfriends to give a crap."

"He's not really dating twelve-year-olds, is he?" I ask, disgusted.

"No, but his newest girlfriend is twenty-one. Three years older than us." Josh caps his straw with his finger and pulls it out of his cup.

"That's pretty gross. From her end, too."

"No kidding. I've seen the man with his shirt off. Middle-age man boobs." Josh shudders.

"But what is it you want? Do you really want your dad hanging around you all the time? Up your butt, telling you to clean your room, brush your teeth, iron your shoes?"

"Well, no, but—"

"I think you just don't want to deal with the fact that we're getting old. Not man-boob old, but old enough. It kind of sucks that we have to, you know, be responsible and stuff, but it's also kind of cool. We get to *be responsible*. For our own lives. Instead of relying on people and being disappointed, we get to rely on ourselves. You can't do that when you're mooching off your dad and playing music in his basement."

"When the band takes off—"

"Yeah, I know. But that could be a really long time. Or not. But what are you going to do until then?"

"I don't know." Josh drips Coke from his straw onto the bunched-up straw wrapper, and it wriggles and grows like a newborn snake. "Can't you and I just drive and drive and pretend like there is no future? We can go to Canada. Mexico. Russia."

"I don't think we can technically drive to Russia," I interject.

"But we can see it from Alaska."

It's truly a gift how Josh can swerve a conversation away from responsibility as easily as he can his own life. That may be fine for him, but I'm kind of looking forward to this new chapter of responsibility in my life. The freedom of my future, in college, in a new state, is more enticing to me than the freedom of a perpetual road trip. Because it's real.

"We need to get back to reality, Josh," I tell him.

"But why?" He looks into my eyes, and I know he's thinking about us. I am, too.

"Because this can't last forever." I know it's true.

At that moment, a voice from the counter calls our order number.

"Pizza's ready." Josh smashes the snake with his palm, and it turns from living creature to wet paper. He slides out of his seat and picks up the pizza. We eat in silence. I watch passersby through the window, then change my focus to the reflection. A windowpane divides my view of me and Josh. My eyes relax, and I watch as our two reflected images float farther and farther apart.

Outside, the sun begins to melt the cold air between me and Josh.

"What do you want to do now?" he asks.

"Maybe we should just go home. Say screw it, and just chalk this up as a road trip. Nothing more."

"No quest?"

"I'm starting to think quests are for knights and dragons and ladies with tall pointy hats hanging out tower windows."

"You could do that, you know. Buy a pointy hat. Hang out a window. I'd save you."

I want to add, "With your dad's credit card?" but that seems harsh. He's just trying to be sweet, and he is.

"Let's ride the dragon over to a cell phone store and buy a charger," Josh says, and takes my hand tentatively. I hold his.

"Technically, I think we're supposed to slay the dragon, not ride it."

"Not in my world." Josh grins. "Now where exactly did we park?"

We walk in the direction from which we think we came, but with a lot of time and distance between us and our parking spot, we end up wandering for almost an hour. We pass a million little shops and eventually find a Radio Shack to sell us a cell phone charger.

Once we're outside, I look at the little plastic bag in Josh's hand. "Now what?"

"Now what what?"

"So we've got a charger, but we don't have a car. Or an outlet."

"Yeah. That could be a glitch."

"You could be a glitch. Who says 'glitch'?"

We laugh. We walk. We pretend that it's just a normal day in a normal city. But the truth floats around the back of my brain, pushing its way to the front. Penny is here somewhere, and I still want to find her.

I envision finding the Eurosport, plugging the phone into the lighter, watching the face light up. Would I instantly call Penny's parents and turn her in? But what happens to her then? What happens when she has to go home and deal with Gavin and her mom and dad? Is Gavin really some abusive psycho? Is her mom really just a QVC-obsessed, self-absorbed bitch? Is anybody *just* one thing? Penny sure isn't. For so long I thought she was just this pathetic soul who needed saving. And then she goes and does this—she didn't just run away or fake her own kidnapping; she made it possible for me and Josh to, well, do whatever it is we're doing. It's hard to be mad at her for that.

I wish I could have found her. Talked to her. Actually heard her side. What she wanted to do, not what she thought other people wanted from her. I wish I could have known who the real Penny is. She's got to be in there somewhere.

My feet are sore and I'm losing steam. We still haven't found our car, although our surroundings do look familiar. Or maybe that's just because we've passed the same corner five times. As we search for the perfect café to rest, through and around Chinatown, we marvel at the full duck bodies hanging in butcher shop windows.

"I prefer my bird as un-poultry-shaped as possible," Josh declares. "Optimal form: nuggets." I nod in agreement, my head heavy from the mass amount of walking and minimal amount of caffeine. My eyes scan the surrounding storefronts, hoping to find our salvation.

Instead of a café, I spy something else. A sign.

"Josh. Look," I say, pointing.

"What? 'Twenty-Four Hour Dry Cleaning'?"

"No. The *other* sign."

Josh reads from a small hanging hand-painted sign on a nearby building: "Twenty-Four Hour Church of Elvis." Elvis has been with us the whole journey. Elvis knows something.

Josh looks at me with a questioning tilt of his head. "Do you think it's a sign?" he asks.

"The sign is a sign." I nod. "We need to go in there. Now."

211

We enter the building, which looks like a regular old office building, and spot a sign indicating the church is on the second floor. I'm usually afraid to use office-building stairwells, worrying about predators lurking in the cinder-block walls. But this time I whip open the door marked EMERGENCY EXIT, and Josh follows me as I run up the stairs with abandon.

The church is clearly marked with an open entry-way, where we see a room filled with multifarious objects, loads of them, displayed haphazardly. I assumed the focus would be all Elvis, all the time, by the name, but the church is crowded with cardboard cutouts of hack movie stars and old instruments, scribbly, unique artwork, and various model heads with wigs. A group of people huddle around an older woman, who by the sound of it, is a wacky tour guide of sorts, explaining the origins of the random artifacts.

This place makes no sense. There's nothing church-like about the room, which reeks of Mars' Cheese Castle char-latanism, while the collection of oddities is reminiscent of a much-smaller-scale House on the Rock. It really is a small world after all.

It gets even smaller when I spy a familiar face among the tour takers. "Penny?" I call incredulously.

CHAPTER TWENTY-FOUR

The person turns around.

And it's her.

It's Penny.

"Lil?" she asks, excited. She runs over and stops in front of me. Her awkward arms say she wants to give or get a hug, but that's not quite how I'm feeling at the moment. "Your hair looks so cool! Ethan said you called. I tried to call you back, but it went straight to voicemail. Did you get my message?"

I'm still in semi-shock that Penny is standing in front of me, and the batty lady and her Elvis tour are starting to freak me out. "Can we get out of here?" I ask Penny. "That woman is giving us the evil eye," which she is, literally, by staring at us and pointing the devil hand sign in our direction.

Penny waves who I assume must be Ethan out of the tour group, and we plod our way down the stairs and outside before saying anything else.

. . .

"So, oh my god, you came here for me?" Penny asks us, and it's like she's not herself. I've never seen her this naturally happy. Real smile. No paranoid side glances. Even her clothes have turned happy: pink capri jeans and a yellow tank. I don't have time to answer her before she says, "Oh! This is Ethan. These are my friends from home, Lil and Josh."

Josh shakes Ethan's hand, and it's the first time I get a look at Ethan. He's tallish, not quite as tall as Josh, but taller than me. Sandy brown hair swayed over his forehead. Sparkly turquoise eyes and a nose that ends in a flat tip. Undeniably and beyond cute. I can feel my cheeks warm when he shakes my hand—great eye contact—and says, "Nice to meet you." Way to go, Penny.

I turn to her, to get the sperm whale in the room (much larger than an elephant) out of the way, and directly ask, "Are we still the only people who know where you are?"

She makes a stupid cutesy face. "Yes. I mean, besides Ethan of course."

Next to me is a free newspaper box, some real estate junk mag, so I take one out, roll it up, and proceed to whack Penny, hard, in the head. Not hard enough to do damage, but hard enough to let her know I'm pissed at the position she's put me in.

"Ow!" she whimpers. "What was that for?"

"Oh, let's see. That one was for your obliviousness. This one"—I hit her again—"is for your dad calling me." *Smack.* "Your mom." *Whack.* "The cops." Penny starts to block the magazine but drops her hands in surprise at the mention of the police.

"The police really called you?" she asks, dumbfounded.

"Yeah. *And* the FBI." I go for an FBI smack, but she manages to block that one. So I hit her hand, which as a result, causes Penny to smack herself in the face. Josh chuckles.

"Wait," Ethan speaks to Penny. "I thought your parents knew you were here. I mean, you used my phone to call them."

Penny makes a guilty face and says, "Pretended to?"

"You really didn't think anyone would follow up on this, seeing as you faked. Your. Own. Kidnapping?" I punctuate the question for maximum emphasis. Will she get it?

"What?" Ethan chokes. "Are you freakin' kidding me? That is messed up." He turns to me.

"Yeah," I agree.

"I'm innocent." Ethan throws his hands up in surrender. "I thought she was just stopping here before she visits her grandma in Vancouver."

"Do you even have a grandmother in Vancouver, Penny?" I ask her.

"Possibly? Do we ever really know who our family is?" She tries to get philosophical on us.

"You are so weird," I point out, but I can't help but smile. It's pretty amazing to see Penny joking. Will that all go away if she calls home and turns herself in? Will Penny turn back into Cinderella before the fairy godmother paid her a visit? Am I her fairy godmother? Is Ethan?

While I battle with my crappy fairy-tale metaphor, Ethan makes my decision for me. "Here." He shoves his phone at Penny. "Call your parents now so they don't call the coast guard or something." The coast guard. Ethan's kind of funny.

"I'm not ready. I don't know what I'd say. What are they going to say? Are they going to be mad at me?" The old tragic Penny pops her sad head into view. I don't want that.

"How about you and I talk a little, and if it's okay with you, Ethan, Josh borrows your phone"—Josh looks at me with a face that says, *Do I have to?*—"he needs to call his dad."

I watch Josh's expression shift from annoyance to resignation when he takes the phone from Ethan. "Thanks, man, I'll only be a minute." Josh steps away from the three of us to gain some privacy. Penny and I walk away from Ethan and sit down on a nearby building's stoop.

Penny is silent, so I start. "So. How's it going?" I try to be casual, hoping that my lack of pressing will inspire

Penny to spill her life's story, complete with actual facts and not just what she thinks I want to hear.

"Okay," is all she says.

"Can I ask you something?" I ask.

"Of course."

"Why did you do it?"

"Which part?"

"I don't know. Run away? Fake it all? Tell me and only me?" My voice goes up in exasperation.

"That's a pretty long story," Penny warns.

"You can tell me the Spark Notes version."

So she does. And in the end, it's even simpler than Spark Notes. Penny was in a hole, and she needed to get out. She couldn't break up with Gavin because she loves him too much, but she couldn't stay with him either. She doesn't explain, and I don't press. She couldn't keep doing what her parents expected of her, but she couldn't tell them no because she never has. The only way out was to get out. But she didn't want anyone to be mad at her, so she staged the kidnapping. And she told me because if she didn't tell someone, she thought no one would even know she was gone.

"People love you, Penny. Your parents. Your bratty sister. Gavin, for better or for worse. How would they not notice you were gone?"

"I just pictured this big homecoming, you know? Hugs and tears and balloons."

"Balloons?" I laugh.

"Yeah. You know. Those really big, expensive shiny ones from the grocery store. I always wanted a bouquet of those. I told Gavin once, but he told me that was retarded."

"Well, it is just a little." I nudge her with my shoulder.

"I'd settle for just one balloon." She sighs.

"Sorry to say, I don't think you'll get one when your parents find out the truth."

"Do I really need to tell them the truth?" She seems so scared again. So the way I used to know her.

"That's up to you. As long as you let them know you're okay, then I'm out of trouble, I guess. You could have given me a police record, you know."

"Damn. Sorry, Lil. But thank you." Penny sniffs a couple times and glances up at me.

I nod a *you're welcome*. I want to tell her thank you, too. For what she's done for me. But if I get into that, then Penny's story seems less important. So I let her thank me. It's something I needed to hear.

About ten minutes pass, when Josh and Ethan walk over to us. Josh thrusts the phone at Penny, and asks, "Ready to spill?"

"No," she answers, but she takes the phone from him and begins dialing. The three of us watch her with anticipation, and I hear a collective breath when Penny ekes out an apprehensive "Mom?"

Ethan, Josh, and I walk away so she can tell her truth. Or not. But as long as they know she's okay, I'm in the clear.

"So . . . ," Ethan begins awkwardly. "You guys are Penny's friends from home?"

"Yep." I nod. "And you're"—I pause, not quite sure where to go with this—"Penny's long-distance—"

Ethan interrupts, "Friend. We're friends. She's been sleeping in my sister's room while she visits."

"Cool. Cool," is all Josh can say. I want to ask him what went down with his dad, but it doesn't seem right in front of someone he barely knows. It's hard enough for Josh to talk about it in front of me, his, well, what am I exactly at this point?

We observe Penny's conversation from a distance, from guilty confession to apology, from insolence to tears, and finally to defeat. I look at Josh for reactions during the call, and he gives me Quest Completed fist pumps. I look at Ethan, and he gives me parental nods of approval. When the conversation's over, we're all exhausted from the enormous weight that's been lifted.

Penny made a deal with her parents to come home and get counseling while she attends a nearby community college. Once she feels better adjusted, she can think about going away to school full-time. And her parents will hire an actual babysitter for Annabelle from now on so that Penny can focus on school and her issues. Those issues, which she admitted may have something to do with Gavin, might mean talking to the police. But her parents assured her they will support her 100 percent. "I don't know if I believe them," Penny says, with the familiar fear and sadness hiding behind her eyes. She's allowed to stay in Portland for a few more days, then she has to fly back, when she will meet with the police to clarify that she was not, indeed, kidnapped. If she comes clean, her parents assured her, she won't have to worry about charges pressed against her. "For eluding the law," she explains.

So that's it. Neatly wrapped up? Not exactly. Penny's parents may just be giving her the balloons and tears she wants now, but who knows if they'll be this forgiving when she gets home. Is it my problem anymore? Was it ever my problem? I look at Penny, at Ethan, at beautiful Josh, and I realize that whatever happens with Penny, she'll figure it out. Life is a big, long journey, with a whole bunch of bumps and twists, and freaky roadside attractions that, no matter what, lead us somewhere. I like it best how Buckaroo Banzai said it in another late-night movie: "Wherever you go, there you are."

Here we are.

CHAPTER TWENTY-FIVE

We pile into Ethan's car, a newer Honda Civic with a license plate holder that reads, FOLLOW ME TO THE LIBRARY—READ. "It's my mom's car," he explains. "She's a librarian."

Our first goal is to find the Eurosport. Once it's located, we'll reward ourselves with coffee.

Ethan drives us up and down one-way streets, until they begin to look familiar. After about twenty minutes, the Eurosport pops into view. We erupt into applause and decide to leave it until later, Ethan writing down the cross streets on an old receipt and stuffing it into the glove compartment. I wonder if he has any pictures in there. And what the heck it means if he does.

Ethan takes us to what he calls "a Portland must," Rimsky-Korsakoffeehouse. From the front, you can barely tell that it's a restaurant, the facade looks so much like the houses nearby. Inside Ethan explains that some of the tables are trick tables, so we stake ourselves out at a normal table and watch other unsuspecting customers look confused as their tables slowly rise or shrink back into the wall. Next, Ethan practically orders Penny and me to go to the bathroom, so we do, and we're in awe of the odd beauty. Legs dangle from the ceiling as though we're viewing them from underwater, and a mermaid offers us toilet paper. Every bit of this place is art.

Our coffee arrives, complete with requisite surly waiter, and it's then that I discover how much Ethan and I have in common. We both have a fascination with historical dead people (which, Josh points out, are "all dead people. Because, if you're dead, you're history." "Shut up" is all I can think of to retort). We both wrote for our high school literary magazines. And the most random item of all is that we'll both be starting at Winthorp College in the fall.

"That's crazy," I say for the umpteenth time over some mango cake dessert. 'Cause it is. Coming all the way to Portland to find a friend who faked her own kidnapping, spending all this time in a car with Josh to finally give me more than just best-friend status, finding several people who knew several people named Ethan, which didn't even matter because we found the right one without using our leads, and that the actual, correct Ethan is this really cute, nice, interesting guy who's going to the same small college as me in the fall?

"Pretty crazy," he agrees. All Josh can do is nod dully in agreement. Do I detect a note of jealousy? I wonder what Josh sees in Ethan? What do I see? And I know what it is. Ethan represents my future, wherever he fits into it. And Josh, well, he most certainly was my past, and is still definitely my present. But can he really fit into that place in my future?

When the check arrives, Josh declares, "Our work here is done." I know he means the restaurant, but the statement is fitting for this whole journey. We found Penny. Josh got the girl. But for how long?

Ethan offers Josh some money, and Josh waves his hand away. "It's on me." *It's on your dad*, I think to say, but it's not as though I have any right to out him. I haven't spent a penny of my bat mitzvah reserves.

We step outside into a cool summer night. Portland seems like a great city, somewhere I'd like to visit under different circumstances. But Josh is right: Our work here is done, and I'm ready to start heading back, to drive our way out of limbo and into our future.

"You guys can crash at my house tonight," Ethan suggests, but we politely decline.

"The old highway's a-callin'," Josh tells him, without me having to say anything. Good ol' Josh and the good ol' road. *Ye Ol' Faithful*, I think, and laugh to myself at the memory. So many miles ago.

As expected, Ethan finds our car without a problem.

There's a ticket on the windshield, but Josh just pulls it off and tosses it on the ground. "It's another state," he explains. "What are they going to do? Come after me?"

"You can at least throw it in the trash," I scold, picking it up off the street.

"Actually, there's a recycling can right over there," Ethan points out. So there is. Josh looks annoyed at being reprimanded by not one, but two people. He rushes through his good-byes to Ethan and Penny with a "See you guys. Thanks for keeping Penny warm," and he waits for me in the car.

I shake Ethan's hand, such an unnatural gesture for me, but I thought contact would be nice and didn't want to overstep with a hug. We exchange phone numbers and email addresses on more receipts from his wallet so we can find each other again before school starts in the fall. For some reason, I don't think I'll have trouble finding Ethan again if I'm meant to. Considering the fatefulness of finding him the first time.

Penny watches me and Ethan, tears pooling under her eyes. I don't know if she's sad to see me go, or if the contact exchange solidifies the fact that there is, indeed, an impending future.

"Have a safe trip," I say to her.

"You, too," she chokes out. "I'll call you when I get home?" she asks, eyes like saucers ready to overflow with tear-drop tea.

"Maybe you should just wait until I call you. I'd sort of like this thing to blow over with your parents and the cops and the FBI. . . ." I stop myself from saying something else about how I'll call once she's got a better handle on reality, but that seems pretty cold. And I don't know if I even feel that way about Penny anymore. Without Penny, I wouldn't be where I'm standing right now. No matter how round-about it was to get here.

We hug good-bye, and I slide into the passenger side of the Eurosport. Ethan and Penny watch as we drive off, so we wave and they wave, and then we're gone.

When we're several blocks away, Josh pulls over. "I wanted to talk to you before we started driving, but it seemed like they were expecting a dramatic exit."

"Yeah," I agree. Josh puts his arm up on my seat, an invitation to be closer. I hesitate, but then think, why not? Right now is right now, and right now it would be nice to sink into Josh's strong shoulder.

"So where are we going?" I ask.

"I was kind of wondering the same thing," he responds, clearing some strands of hair away from my eyes. I don't look at him, but I take in his delicious smell. We're still nowhere, I think. Even though we are headed back home, we still have a journey to get there. So I kiss his cheek gently. "Why don't we just go?" I say. "Because we're going to get where we're going no matter what." I try to be mystical and vague, but—

"Yeah. That doesn't really make sense." Josh smiles and shakes his head.

"Not so much," I agree, and while I try and formulate something more clever, Josh leans in to kiss me. It's not a long kiss, but it takes effect on me like a temporary love potion. "I wonder what it would be like if we just drove forever? Like you said, going where the road takes us, living off your father's credit card?"

"My dad says I have one week left on the credit card, and then he's cutting it up," Josh tells me. I'm surprised at how he doesn't sound that mad.

"That's still a week, right?"

"Yeah. It is." He smiles at me, the most melting grin. "He also said he'd pay for a month in a studio, a real studio, so I can record a demo. He'll even help me with some connections his friends have. But I still have to get a job until something real happens."

"Something real will happen. It's not like you're going to fake your own kidnapping, right?"

"Yeah, who would be stupid enough to do that?"

"How about for now we just pretend that the future doesn't exist, and we are only where we are right now, and if we stop going wherever it is that we may be headed, that the future is actually going to get here sooner rather than later."

Josh pauses before he laughs out a "What?"

"All I'm saying is, start the car, Josh."

• • •

*I did it. It didn't happen the way I thought. But that was
okay. I screwed up royally, but I did it. I did something. I
did something right. My way. People thought I was really
kidnapped. People cared enough to call the police. The FBI.
To follow me. The sucky thing is that I have to go back.
But after that, after I appease the parents, straighten some
stuff out, maybe I can leave again. I can get away and find
other people who like to be around me and I like to be around.
Maybe I'll go back to Portland and get a job or go to school.
Maybe I'll go to Hawaii and work on a beach somewhere.
Even in a bikini.*

*I talked to Gavin. Ethan sat next to me and held my hand. I
told Gavin I needed some time apart. He yelled at me and told
me I was a moron for running away and now the police are
calling him. I told him I was sorry. I didn't mean to hurt him.
Did he mean to hurt me? Then he got quiet. I love you,
Penny, he said. I love you, too, Gavin, I said. Maybe I'll see
you when you get home, he said. Maybe. I have to think
about it. Talk to someone about it. Maybe. And we hung up.
And I cried on Ethan's shoulder until I choked like a little kid.*

*I go home tomorrow. My mom promised that she'd have bal-
loons waiting for me. I believe her.*

227

CHAPTER TWENTY-SIX

Josh and I use the entire allotted credit-card week to get home. I charge my phone, text my mom, and then we turn it off to make this a true road trip. Our drive takes us through more towns with names like Walla Walla and Garryowen, which remind us of the multiple-named girls of Pendleton. "How many years ago was that?" Josh jokes, but I agree that time, along with Elvis, has left the building.

Devils Tower, Hells Canyon, Flaming Gorge—sometimes it sounds like we're headed to the ends of the earth. That's working just fine for us.

We spend a night at an EconoLodge and stay up way too late watching episodes of *The Golden Girls*, and spend a day gawking with the tourists at Mount Rushmore, which we both decide looks like a movie set. "Isn't that Nicolas Cage up there?" Josh squints, and we waste a good twenty minutes staring at a spot on top of Roosevelt's head. Passersbys join us, without asking what we're looking at.

Next we head to Crazy Horse, a Native American monument being blown into the side of a mountain, in the vein of Mount Rushmore, but with a real founding father. So far, all that's really completed is Crazy Horse's face and the top of his arm, but it already looks impressive. "I wonder if they'll ever finish," I say.

"The guy who started it refused money from the government," Josh reads from a pamphlet. "He never expected it to be finished in his lifetime."

"Nor in mine," I say.

"Come on. This guy had a vision. And he wasn't deterred by the restraints of time or money," Josh philosophizes. I know he's thinking about his own time and money constraints, his own vision, but I don't want him to get stuck in those thoughts.

"I'm having a vision now, too," I say with mystical eyes. "Of a bacon double cheeseburger." So we head to the concession stand without any more thought of what's to come.

Our last stop before the inevitable reality road home is in Austin, Minnesota, at the Spam Museum. Yes, the canned meat Spam. Surprisingly, it's not a tin can display, but a state-of-the-art pop show of snacks, and we gorge ourselves on their endless supplies of free samples. Even though we have more than enough T-shirts to last us through another week of road trip, we both pick up Spam shirts. "For you to wear at college, so you don't forget me," Josh says, and a little more reality sneaks its way in.

That night, in a king-size bed at a Comfort Inn hotel, Josh and I extend the night recounting our favorites: favorite doughnut, favorite gas station attendant, favorite rest-stop bathroom. "Your breath smells like Spam," I tell Josh.

"Yours smells like roses. Roses watered with Spam juice," he tells me.

I dream of Nicolas Cage eating processed meat, as I'm enveloped in Josh's arms.

We arrive back in Suburbia around two in the afternoon. I half expect the town to look completely different, transformed into the Town of the Future. Or crumbling from years of neglect. But the only thing that looks different is that the bright green grass of early summer has browned into the dry, trampled grass of midsummer. In a few weeks, I'll start packing my belongings for the drive to Winthorp with Mom. In a few weeks, Josh will have to start looking for a job. Or get famous so he doesn't have to.

The Eurosport pulls into my driveway. I called my mom yesterday to let her know I'd be home. She had to work today, so I'll see her later tonight. We planned a welcome-home pizza dinner, Chicago style, of course.

Josh shuts off the engine. "So," he says.

"So," I agree, and I remember our "Hi," "Hi" conversation. We sit in the car, the past, present, and future waiting for us outside the protective Eurosport doors. Runaway saved. Monuments admired. Thousands of miles covered. It's all too much. Tears uncontrollably stream down my cheeks.

"Hey, hey." Josh slides into me and pulls my head onto his shoulder, stroking my hair, the red now faded from the sun. "It's OK. Everything's great, right?" He kisses the top of my head.

"I don't want to get out of the car," I sniff. "When I do, it's all going to change."

"No, it won't," Josh says, and he kisses away a tear. "You'll still exist, and I'll still exist, and this summer, no matter how over it gets, will always exist. It's of history, right?" I bob my head in agreement. "You know what else we'll always have?" he asks.

A list runs through my head. A kiss? Our love? The cell phone charger?

"A T-shirt that says, 'Cheese makes it taste better,'" he answers.

That we will. I can wear it as I walk around campus at school. While I'm writing stories for class. When I meet Ethan for coffee?

"Yeah." I smile. "We'll always have cheese shirts."

"They should put *that* on a T-shirt," he declares.

"I'd buy it," I say.

We're quiet for a few minutes.

"I wonder who spray painted the rocks," I say. It hadn't crossed my mind before.

"Someone very wise, I reckon."

"You reckon, huh?" I laugh.

"That I do."

I inhale Josh's dirty T-shirt smell and burn it into my scent memory. I trace his lip with my finger to memorize the touch. I look at his eyes, and find the one fleck of gold in the brown. I close my eyes to save it all.

"Josh?" I finally say, my eyes changing focus from Josh's face to the bug smush on the windshield.

"Yes, Lil?"

I take a deep breath, and slowly let my eyes adjust to the world beyond the bugs. "It's time to open the doors."

At the same time, Josh and I break open the seal of our summer and step out into our future.

GO FISH

JULIE HALPERN

© Matthew Cordell

What did you want to be when you grew up?

I don't think I knew as a kid. In junior high, we had to do a presentation on a profession, something we might want to be, but part of the project was to interview someone. I was too shy to find someone in an actual field of interest, so I interviewed my mom's friend, an accountant. I think I went with that for one or two more career assignments. At the end of high school, I wanted to go into film, which was one of my college majors. But after interning on *The Adventures of Pete & Pete* and having a total blast, I realized the business side of it wasn't for me. I eventually ended up with a master's degree in Library and Information Science and was a school librarian for ten years before I left to write and stay home with my daughter. I may go back to being a librarian someday. It was really fun.

What were your hobbies as a kid? What are your hobbies now?

Is watching TV a hobby? I watched way too much TV as a kid. My childhood was when home computers were just starting to take off, so I really got into our Apple 2GS. I made banners and newspapers and played "Where in the World Is Carmen Sandiego?" Now? I still like computer games, although as a parent, it's pretty much impossible to find the time to play them. And I like to plan vacations, even if I have no money to take them.

How did you celebrate publishing your first book?
I don't remember what happened when *Get Well Soon* came out, but I do remember when I talked to my editor while I was at work, and she told me they wanted to acquire my book. I ran out from my office into the school library and said, "My book is going to be published!" There were two kids in the library, and they appeased me with the slow clap. Very triumphant.

Where do you write your books?
At this point, wherever I can. I can't write with any noise, so I try to book a private room at the public library when I have a deadline. But most days, I'm too busy with my kids to do that, so I will write with earplugs in when I find time. I wrote half of *The F- It List* while sitting in the car while my youngest was in preschool.

What was your best friend like in high school?
The character of Tracy from *Get Well Soon* is very much based on my best friend from high school—auto shop, shortness, professional wrestling, and all. When I wrote her as a book character, I was reminded of how hilarious the real person actually was (and still is)!

Who was your favorite teacher in high school?
I had an English teacher who ran a philosophy club, which I thought was cool. He took the club to a horror movie con-

ference at a neighboring high school, and that kind of changed my life in terms of film knowledge. I also had a gym teacher I really liked; he never made me feel bad for being an out-of-shape runner. Plus, he had this ridiculous routine where he'd play Hulk Hogan's theme song to get us pumped up before a run. I wish I had included that in the book!

What's your idea of fun?
I like going places—museums, comic book conventions, Renaissance fairs, jelly bean factories (all places I go on a regular basis)—with my family.

What's your favorite song?
"The Door into Summer" by the Monkees.

Who is your favorite fictional character?
Buffy Summers from *Buffy the Vampire Slayer*.

What was your favorite book when you were a kid? Do you have a favorite book now?
Mouse Tales by Arnold Lobel. It is still my favorite book. ". . . And what nice new feet you have." Could there be anything better?

What's your favorite TV show?
Of all time, it would be the original Degrassi series from the late 80s/90s, *Buffy the Vampire Slayer*, *Beverly Hills 90210* (also the original), and *Battlestar Galactica* (the newer version). Currently, I'm really into *Supernatural*.

If you could travel anywhere in the world, where would you go and what would you do?
I would go back to Australia, with my family this time. I lived there and traveled all around after college, and I learned so much. I felt a real connection to the red earth, the animals, the people, the history, and even the spiders. They have A LOT of spiders.

If you could travel in time, where would you go and what would you do?
I would go to the 1893 World's Columbian Exposition in Chicago. That makes me sound much more old-fashioned than I actually am, but something about the wonder and the newness of so many things, especially in my beloved home-town, has always seemed really magical to me.

What advice do you wish someone had given you when you were younger?
I don't know if I would have listened to anyone's advice when I was younger, so it probably wouldn't have mattered if they gave it to me.

Do you ever get writer's block? What do you do to get back on track?
I don't. Not that everything I write is easy and stellar, but I just try to write anything—even if it's the character going to the bathroom. At least I'm moving the story along, among other things. . . .

If you were a superhero, what would your superpower be?
Flight. Airplane rides can be pretty excruciating.

What do you wish you could do better?
Break-dance.

What do you want readers to remember about your books?
Everybody is weird in some way.

ALEX BUCKLEY is not having a great year. Her father just died, her best friend, Becca, slept with her boyfriend, and she can't seem to open up to Leo, the guy she's had a crush on for years. Then she finds out that Becca has cancer, and Alex vows to help Becca fulfill her bucket list before it's too late. It's the least a best friend can do.

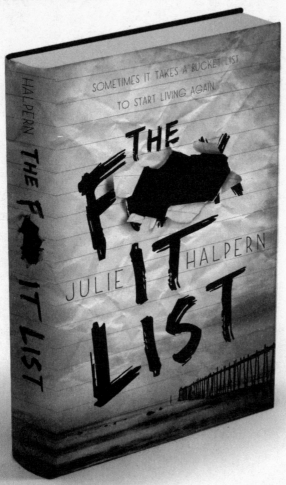

KEEP READING FOR A SNEAK PEEK OF

CHAPTER 1

THE ONLY THING WORSE than having my best friend sleep with my boyfriend the night of my father's funeral would be if she killed my dad herself. Becca didn't, which was the one thing that redeemed her. Still, I allowed myself the entire summer after the trampful event to be mad at her.

It's not as though I haven't done shitty things to Becca. In third grade, I announced in front of our whole class that she would never make the lead in the school play because she had boy hair. Which she did. Kind of forward-thinking of her for a third grader, although it was probably her mom's choice after the Lice Crisis of Room 143. In junior high I managed to leak the fact that she stuffed her bra when a tuft of tissues fell out of her shirt, and I yelled down the hall, "Becca! I think one of your boobs fell out!" And just last year, even though I swore everyone already knew, I let slip that she lost her virginity to her second cousin the night of her Bat Mitzvah. All of the above seemed unforgivable at the times of occurrence, and yet she forgave me.

Just like I forgave her for stealing my thunder as Mary Todd Lincoln in the fourth-grade play by accepting the lead male role of Honest Abe. After that, the entire play went drag, and Becca was hailed the class comedian. I quickly learned I preferred being behind the scenes, anyway. I also forgave the time she announced I had my period in sixth grade by asking in front of the alpha girls if that's why I took so long in the bathroom. And the time freshman year when she accidentally shredded my twelve-page English essay because she thought they were pages of my pathetic attempt at a vampire novel she needed to rid the world of.

Best friends forgive each other. And I knew I'd forgive her for screwing Davis. Eventually. It's not like he was my one true love or anything. We had only gone out for a month before my dad was killed in a cab on his way home from the airport. Davis and I didn't talk until two days after the news of my dad went around. I had to call *him* to get some sympathy. Maybe if I'd had sex with him, he would have called sooner. But there was something about him that turned me off. He was always listening to misogynistic rap songs with ridiculous lyrics, like, "With my nuts on your tonsils."

"Sick." I reacted to the lyrics.

"What?" he asked incredulously. He was always incredulous.

"Dude, that's like me saying, 'With my ovaries on your uvula.'"

"Is my uvula near my johnson?"

It wasn't worth an answer. It was just one of those lazy boyfriend situations because I was bored while Becca was off starring in the school musical, and Davis was always around. Plus, he had a car. At first, his long, wavy hair and busted-up knuckles from working his dad's deck-sanding business were a turn-on. But the thought of his nuts on my tonsils? Not so much.

It's not like Becca slept with guys all the time, although losing her virginity to her second cousin at the ripe old age of thirteen made it sound like she did. He wasn't a blood relative; there were divorces and remarriages. And he was older and super hot, plus there was Manischewitz wine involved. It was stupid, she was mortified, and lucky for her the only consequence was the agonizing guilt and residual slut label that hung around for a couple of years. That wore off once we hit high school and other people really started sleeping around.

And it's not like Becca didn't give me a good reason for the sexual mishap with Davis. Becca loved my dad. I did, too, of course, but Becca had never had a real dad in her life, so she idolized mine. Her parents divorced when she was one, and all Becca knew from men were her mom's grotesque attempts at finding fatherly replacements. Becca preferred my dad, a constant and caring male authority figure. Since we were little, he sort of became my designated parent while Mom attempted to wrangle my younger twin brothers, AJ and CJ. (Our family likes to shorten names as much as possible, so Andrew Jacob and Charles Joshua became AJ and CJ, and I went from Alexandra Judith to Alex, occasionally Al.) Dad took me and Becca to parks, zoos, museums, and restaurants throughout our childhood. As we got older and the twins became more outdoorsy, Dad broke out the camping equipment and fishing poles. I preferred camping in front of the TV, but Dad was still the go-to parent for talks. Becca even somehow managed to share in my first big sex talk from Dad, which went something like this, "You go near a boy's penis, it better be wearing a condom." Dad was frank and realistic about things, which is where I got it. He wasn't afraid of his daughter going out and experiencing things. At least, he never showed it. Like when I told him I really wanted to study film when I head off to college, he didn't try to convince me to go into something more practical, like Mom.

"You're so good with numbers, Alex. You could be a math teacher. Or an accountant." Mom was sweet, but way serious about life. Dad always said life was too short to be serious.

I wish he wasn't right about that.

While I huddled with my mom and the twins at the funeral, Becca was in Davis's backseat drowning her sorrows between her legs.

She told me about it, which was *something*. When the funeral ended, and we went back to our house for shivah, Becca busted in the door bawling her eyes out. It wasn't beyond Becca to milk any situation for drama (she was well known for her crying-on-cue abilities), but this was over the top. She dragged me by my black-sleeved arm up the stairs of our house, so I grabbed for a tissue and thrust it at her. Instead of taking the tissue, she dove into me and cried between gulps and heaves, "I'm so sorry, Alex. So so sorry."

"I know. It's horrible. But you didn't kill him. Stop. You're crying more than I am."

That drove her into another crying jag that lasted a good five minutes, complete with hiccups. I was all cried out from hospital visits and coffin choosing, so I lay down on my bed and stared at the green-tinted, glow-in-the-dark stars on my ceiling. Becca, of course, helped me affix those back in sixth grade.

When she managed to calm herself and finally took advantage of the tissue, she whispered with a look of wide-eyed horror, "I slept with Davis."

I didn't say anything, unsure whether she meant they just took a nap together. Like, how the word "ridiculous" can be good or bad.

"In the back of his car," she continued, and the meaning cleared up.

"What? Why?" My empty stomach tensed into an even larger knot than had already rested there from my dad's death.

"I'm sorry, Alex, it just hurts so much, and I felt so alone because I'm not really part of your family and Davis drove me to the funeral and we smoked some pot in his car—"

"What?" Becca and I were anti, so that was a double "what?" One of our favorite party pastimes was insulting people who drank or smoked because they were too insecure to show their real selves. Unlike us, we thought superiorly.

"I didn't know what to do. He offered, and I thought it would make things feel not so bad, and then I just felt sleepy and he was so close and I was wearing a skirt with no tights because it was too hot—"

"TMI, Becca. Stop before he inserts his penis."

She laughed because it did sound absurd. But she wasn't allowed to laugh. She was my best friend. My dad just died. And she slept with my boyfriend. Who I had planned to break up with anyway, but still.

"I can't deal with this now." I stood up. "There are people downstairs waiting for me."

"I'm really sorry." The tears tumbled out of her eyes again, but all I could do was give her an exhausted glare.

"Don't call me, okay? Don't text or email or smoke signal or anything. I need some space right now."

"Are you breaking up with me?" she choked.

"I just need us to take a break. I don't need something else to deal with." I stood up without another look at Becca and walked back downstairs to accept the trays of deli food and hugs of sympathy from everyone who knew and loved my dad.

That was the beginning of June and the end of our junior year. Becca called, texted, emailed, messaged, left notes in my mailbox, and sent a muffin basket. It was all duly noted in my mind, but I meant what I said. I needed some space and time to process the summer of shit I had ahead of me. Mourning the loss of my dad, helping my mom with two middle-school brothers, and working at Cellar Subs was all I could handle. I steered clear of social situations, unless they involved family, and I dove deeper into watching horror films as inspiration for a movie I planned to make someday.

The first day of senior year, the plan was to head straight to Becca's locker and tell her, "Okay, I'm over it." Then hug her and never look back.

Only it didn't happen that way. Because Jenna Brown, a peripheral friend who was fun because of her song-parody-writing abilities but also lame because of her obsession with weight loss, waited for me by my locker. When she saw me, she offered her arms in a sympathetic hug. I assumed the gesture was about my dad, which I had hoped was already so last year, when she said, "Oh, Alex, I'm so sorry about Becca."

"It was just a fight. I'm over it. What's to be sorry about?"

"You don't know?" She backed off the hug and looked at me with concern.

"Know what? What happened to Becca?" My heart leaped. Was she dead, too?

"I thought you'd know, since you guys are best friends—"

"Yes, yes, and she fucked my boyfriend. The end. What the hell is wrong with her?"

The problem with being friends with so many people from the drama department was that there was always drama. I had no patience for games of communication. Jenna looked around, frazzled, so I grabbed her shoulders and shook. "What. The. Fuck. Happened. To. Becca?"

She looked genuinely terrified, like I was going to bite off her ear. Which I actually felt like doing. She managed to eke out the worst string of words I'd heard since my dad died. And all of them before that day, too.

"Becca has cancer."

Find these books and find yourself.

Read all the Julie Halpern books.